MONTANA MAVERICKS

Welcome to Big Sky Country, home of the Montana Mavericks! Where free-spirited men and women discover love on the range.

THE ANNIVERSARY GIFT

The mayor of Bronco and his wife have invited the whole town to help celebrate their thirtieth anniversary, but when the pearl necklace the mayor bought his wife goes missing at the party, it sets off a chain of events that brings together some of Bronco's most unexpected couples. Call it coincidence, call it fate—or call it what it is: the power of true love to win over the hardest cowboy hearts!

The rancher and the wedding singer. One comes from money, the other...not so much. One enjoys his freedom; the other is soon to be a mom. There are many reasons they shouldn't be together, but logic flies out the window whenever they're in each other's orbit. Can love really conquer all?

Dear Reader,

At thirty-five, wealthy rancher Theo Abernathy is finally ready to settle down and find himself a wife. Problem is, all his dates seem to bring up babies and children and families, and Theo is far from ready to be a father. So when he finds himself inexplicably smitten with a four-months-pregnant wedding singer, Theo does his best to ignore his blazing attraction to Bethany McCreery.

About to be a single mother, Bethany can't afford to fall for a man who doesn't want children *now*. They shake on friendship, but Bethany longs for more... Little do they both know that many surprises are in store for them in Bronco this summer.

I hope you enjoy Theo and Bethany's romance. I love to hear from readers, so feel free to email me at MelissaSenate@yahoo.com and check out my website for information on new books coming up.

Happy reading!

Melissa Senate

A LULLABY FOR THE MAVERICK

MELISSA SENATE

Harlequin

MONTANA MAVERICKS

Special thanks and acknowledgment are given to Melissa Senate for her contribution to the Montana Mavericks: The Anniversary Gift miniseries.

Harlequin®
MONTANA MAVERICKS

Recycling programs for this product may not exist in your area.

ISBN-13: 978-1-335-59479-2

A Lullaby for the Maverick

Harlequin Enterprises ULC
22 Adelaide St. West, 41st Floor
Toronto, Ontario M5H 4E3, Canada
www.Harlequin.com

Printed in Lithuania

MIX
Paper | Supporting responsible forestry
FSC® C021394

Melissa Senate has written many novels for Harlequin and other publishers, including her debut, *See Jane Date*, which was made into a TV movie. She also wrote seven books for Harlequin Special Edition under the pen name Meg Maxwell. Her novels have been published in over twenty-five countries. Melissa lives on the coast of Maine with her teenage son; their rescue shepherd mix, Flash; and a lap cat named Cleo. For more information, please visit her website, melissasenate.com.

Books by Melissa Senate

Harlequin Special Edition

Dawson Family Ranch

Santa's Twin Surprise
The Cowboy's Mistaken Identity
Seven Birthday Wishes
Snowbound with a Baby
Triplets Under the Tree
The Rancher Hits the Road

Furever Yours

A New Leash on Love
Home is Where the Hound Is

Montana Mavericks: The Lonelyhearts Ranch

The Maverick's Baby-in-Waiting

Montana Mavericks: The Real Cowboys of Bronco Heights

The Most Eligible Cowboy

Montana Mavericks: Brothers & Broncos

One Night with the Maverick

Visit the Author Profile page
at Harlequin.com for more titles.

Chapter One

As a wedding singer, Bethany McCreery had performed at many June weddings—it was her band's busiest month. From the fanciest Saturday night shindigs to casual afternoon backyard ceremonies, Bethany and her band performed her slow ballads and dance numbers in the midst of all that love, all that happiness and hope for the future. But tonight, June 28, was her favorite wedding of all: her brother Jake's. After all he'd been through, she was so happy that he'd found his forever love. The ceremony had been so touching, and now Bethany stood on the makeshift stage at the reception, held in the beautifully decorated backyard of the bride's grandmother's house.

As Bethany sang a ballad, one of Jake's favorite songs, she watched her brother and his new wife, Elizabeth Hawkins, slow dance. The newlyweds were gazing at each other with such tenderness that Bethany felt her eyes get misty. And she'd cried plenty already during the ceremony. The couple, both widowed, had five children between them, from five to ten years old, and they were now one very big, very happy family.

As she watched her nieces and nephews do an adorable line dance to their own beat, robot moves and ballerina twirls among them, all she could think was, *The five of you will soon have a new cousin.* A baby cousin.

Bethany's baby.

She was four months pregnant.

And no one knew.

Not her mother, with whom she was very close.

Not her brother, who'd always been her best friend.

Not her two close girlfriends, Suzanna and Dana, who she usually told *everything.*

Not even the baby's father, whom she'd intended to tell. Rexx had quit the band not long after their unexpected one-night stand, and when she'd called to tell him about the pregnancy, he'd interrupted her to remind her he was now engaged, so it was best that Bethany not call again. *Click.*

Given her hormones, her nerves, and all the happily-ever-after in the air, no wonder she was extra emotional.

Bethany sang on, gripping the microphone, and moved across the stage, once again noticing the very handsome man who'd been watching her—intently—all night. He stood by the bar, nursing what looked like whiskey. He was looking straight at her. With interest in his eyes. *Yeah, that'll last,* she thought with bittersweet cynicism. *Once you find out I'm pregnant, you won't look my way again.*

Which was fine with her.

Bethany, thirty-five years old, was done with romance, done with love, done with wishing and hoping and wanting.

And she knew who the man was—a very wealthy rancher from a big and influential family here in Bronco, Montana. Theo Abernathy. He was the same age she was, so she'd grown up with him. Theo had had a lot of gorgeous, busty girlfriends with amazing bodies over the years.

Bethany had the busty part down—she'd gone up a cup size already—but her once-svelte figure was changing before her eyes, Bethany marveling at it in the mirror every morning. She loved her new curves, particularly the one on her belly. She was just starting to show, but her penchant for flowy dresses had kept her secret safe. Even her bridesmaid dress had helpful tiers.

Where were you five months ago, Theo Abernathy? she thought with more of that bittersweet cynicism, the yearning and passion in her voice as she sang reminding her what she'd wanted so badly.

A man in her life. A husband. A family.

Now she'd have the family. Just not the man. Or the husband.

Love had passed her by. That was mostly her fault too.

As she sang the closing note, she noticed Theo finishing his drink and setting the glass on a passing waiter's tray. He was moving now—closer to the stage. And closer still, his gaze not leaving hers.

A line of goose bumps broke out on her neck.

She swallowed and put the microphone back on its stand and thanked the audience, sweeping a hand toward the men guys who made up her band, Bethany and the Belters. The guests heartily clapped, and there were even a few wolf whistles, including from the groom.

Theo was still watching her, still inching closer.

Oh, yes, Theo Abernathy had *I'm very interested in you* written all over his handsome face.

Even if he didn't run for the hills when he found out she was pregnant, this was hardly the time to start a romance. She needed to focus on the fact that her life was about to change. Dramatically. She needed to prepare—mentally and emotionally—which for her meant making a lot of lists. Such as people in her life she could count on—and thankfully, there were many. And things she needed from the get-go, like a bassinet, an infant car seat, a stroller, baby bottles, a bath contraption, and *a lot* of diapers. Tiny pajamas and ever tinier socks. Depending on what she was reading, she also needed everything from a baby bouncer to a wipes warmer. And since she'd be a single mother, she'd have to make a new budget and be very careful.

She wouldn't speak for all wedding singers, but Bethany wasn't exactly rolling in dough. She earned enough to pay her bills and had a very small nest egg that would get smaller and smaller even if she spent on just the necessities.

In other words, she was busy, preoccupied, and a bundle of nerves.

And she was something else: deeply happy and fulfilled that she was going to be a mother. When she got scared about the unknown, she'd focus on that. The baby coming.

Bethany forced her gaze off the very hot rancher. She again thanked the clapping guests, announced that the band would be taking a half-hour break, and then headed to the bar—for cranberry juice. With a lime twist that she'd been inexplicably craving for the past few songs.

"You sing like an angel," a male voice said from behind her.

Her drink in hand, she turned to find Theo Abernathy looking at her with that same interest in his green eyes. Ooh boy, was he good-looking. He was very tall, rancher muscular—though as part of the wealthy Abernathy family, did he actually lift bales of hay? She doubted that. His thick, dark hair was tousled back. And his gray suit fit the way expensive custom suits did.

"I felt that last song right here," he added, tapping his well-muscled chest over his heart.

Wow, did he know how to lay it on. And it was working. She felt his compliment in that exact spot in her *own* chest.

Hormones.

"Bethany McCreery, right?" he asked with a sexy smile.

That he knew her name was no surprise, even though they'd never run in the same circles, starting with kindergarten, when he'd sat behind her. But in Bronco, everyone knew everyone.

She eyed his Stetson and smiled at a memory, of Theo being sent to the principal's office the first day of kindergarten because he'd come wearing a cowboy hat—yes, a pricey Stetson at five years old—and had refused to take it off.

"Right," she said. "And you're Theo Abernathy."

"We were in a lot of classes together over the years," he said. "I wonder why we never dated."

She almost snorted. *I'll tell you why. You were a golden boy from one of the richest families in town, and my dad was a truck driver and my mom a secretary at Bronco Bank and Trust for thirty-five years.* Very different circles.

"I wasn't much of a dater back then," she said instead.

She took a sip of her cranberry juice to break eye contact with the man. Way too intense.

"What about now?" he asked, those green eyes twinkling—and intent on her.

She almost spit out her juice. She hadn't expected that.

"I'm taking a break from men," she blurted, feeling her cheeks warm. She hadn't exactly meant to say that. But it was better than the truth: *I'm unlucky in love. And pregnant.*

"Yeah, I've had those breaks. The last woman I dated gave me an ultimatum on our third date—exclusivity *and* assurance that I wanted two children, as she did."

Well, that had her ears perked. "And neither was in your plans?" Bethany asked.

"Honestly, I'm all for exclusivity. I'm thirty-five and have been ready to settle down for a while now. But the children part…that's less a sure thing."

She stared at him. "You don't want kids?"

"I'm sure I do, *someday*. I just don't feel ready yet. That's a lot of responsibility, a lot of sacrifice."

Ah, the thirty-five-year-old man not having to worry about his biological clock. Humph.

And she noticed he didn't mention money—how *expensive* kids were. Because he didn't have to give the cost of raising children a second thought.

"Commitment, yes," he continued with a firm nod. "But a family, the whole shebang? No." He gave his head a shake for emphasis.

Despite Theo's insistence that he was not open to romance, something inside her deflated.

So they were opposites. She was closed to romance but open to children. He was open to romance but closed to children—for now, anyway. And now was key for Bethany.

Wasn't that always the way?

Maybe just in her world.

Luckily, the bartender came over to take Theo's order, which gave her a minute to compose herself, get back to neutral.

His top-shelf scotch in hand, he held it up to her. "To your beautiful voice," he said. "I could listen to you sing all day."

Well, that was nice. She smiled and clinked her glass with his, then took a sip of her cranberry juice.

She was about to make an excuse to slip away, but a group of guests coming to the bar forced him to move closer to her—and he'd been just inches away to start with. They were *so* close that she could smell his cologne or aftershave—faint but spicy. And intoxicating. She was mesmerized.

"As a wedding singer," he said, "this must be your busy season—summer."

She nodded. "The band and I have performed at four-teen weddings this month alone. Everything from Bronco's fanciest venues to barns and even a mountain cave. That was some schlep getting our mikes and drum kit there."

He chuckled. "How were the acoustics?"

"Terrible. But the bride and groom met on a cave ex-ploration trip for singles, so…" She smiled, recalling how dressed up they'd been too—a tux and a ball gown. She'd half expected them to turn up in cargo pants and hiking boots to say their I dos.

She was about to tell him that she had two more wed-dings booked—one in a restaurant and one outdoors on a ranch—which would end June on a very good financial note, when she felt a flutter on the side of her belly.

She almost gasped as her hand flew to the spot. Could it be her baby's first kick? She'd asked her ob-gyn when she could expect that and was told closer to twenty-five weeks with a first pregnancy, but her little one gave her an early little kick.

And reminded her that chatting flirtatiously with Theo Abernathy wasn't how she should be spending her thirty-minute break. The last thing she needed to add to her plate was a silly crush on a man who didn't want kids *now*.

It was bad enough she was charmed by the way his crow's-feet crinkled at the corners of his eyes when he smiled. How broad his shoulders were. The warm intensity of his green eyes.

Plus, she was aware that he was checking her out the way people did when they were definitely interested. The way she was checking *him* out. And what if he noticed her baby bump? She moved her hand, lest she draw attention to her belly.

Not that he'd say, *Oh, you're pregnant.*

So far, no one had. But she knew the town's nosy Nellies would soon enough. Her own family included. She'd tell them before they could notice, of course.

That day was coming up fast. She just hadn't been ready to share the big news yet.

It was definitely time to slip away from Theo. He'd surely feel funny for flirting with a pregnant woman whom he'd just told he didn't want kids in the near future.

"Well," she said, clearing her throat, "I, um, should get back to the stage."

"You have at least fifteen minutes till you're due back on," he pointed out. "I was hoping for a dance—or two or three."

Whoa. If she'd been flattering herself that he was interested, she knew without a doubt now that he was.

The music, via Bluetooth speaker, was another slow love song. A little too romantic. She couldn't be in this man's arms for a minute and a half.

Besides, she needed a chair, pronto. And a back rub that she'd have to provide herself.

"Actually," she said, "I was hoping to find the waiter carrying around the tray of those delicious-looking hors d'oeuvres, the little mushroom tarts. I'm starving, and I've got another two hours of singing ahead of me."

He tilted his head slightly, as if he wasn't used to a woman turning him down for anything, let alone a slow dance.

Trust me, she thought. *I'm saving you.*

Just then, that very waiter happened to be walking by, and Theo stopped him so that they could both put a few of the tiny tarts onto little plates. Two seats at the bar suddenly became vacant, and he gestured toward them. She gave an inward sigh and sat down. He sat beside her and popped a tart in his mouth.

Well, if they were going to talk, she had to steer the conversation to less personal topics. She took a long sip of her juice to give her a few seconds to come up with something.

Ah. Got it, she thought.

"I heard your podcast the other day," she said. "My brother picked me up to go cummerbund shopping, and he was listening to *This Ranching Life*. It was so interesting— and I've never been part of the ranching world. I was hanging on your every word."

The episode had been "a day in the life of a rancher," but wasn't about Theo or the Abernathys or their ranch, the Bonnie B. He'd had a guest, a young cowgirl who'd struggled to get her start on a big cattle ranch, having been turned down for the job by six ranches. "The last foreman told me I'd have to take up bodybuilding before he'd let me step foot on his operation," she'd said. "And then I picked up a hay bale and lifted it over my head. I got the job." Bethany had actually clapped right there in her brother's pickup.

The podcast, which aired weekly, was very popular, not just in town but across the Northwest. Theo had some major sponsors, which she knew from the commercials— rodeos, a chain of feed stores, and some dude ranches, to name a few. Her brother had told her that Theo actually donated all revenue from *This Ranching Life* to a fund for ranchers in need. That sure was nice of him, despite the fact that he was super rich and didn't need the money.

"Wow, that's quite the compliment," Theo said with a smile. "Thanks."

"After listening, I even told my brother I wished I could buy a couple of goats or some chickens," she said with a chuckle. "But I live in a small two-bedroom apartment above a hair salon in Bronco Valley, and *one* goat wouldn't even fit on my tiny balcony. And the chickens would fly away."

He studied her for a moment, and she wondered what he thought about where she lived. She knew he and most of his many siblings lived in luxe cabins at the Bonnie B ranch. His kitchen was probably bigger than her entire apartment.

"It's odd that we've known each other our whole lives but have never really talked," he said. "I've seen you perform at a few other weddings over the years. But this is the first time I've been able to approach you."

Interesting. "Oh? Why is that?"

"Either I had a date or I was on one of my own breaks from anything to do with romance," he said. "But now, neither is the case."

"It is for me," she reminded him.

He tilted his head again. "Ah, right—you're not dating

now. Maybe I can change your mind," he added with a sexy smile.

I doubt I could change yours about children in the next five months, she thought with a sigh.

It was beyond time to make that getaway. She made a show of glancing at her delicate gold watch, a gift from her late grandmother for her sixteenth birthday. "Oh—I'd better get back on stage. Nice to talk to you, Theo." She gave him a tight smile and then hurried toward the stage.

One of two things would happen: either Theo Abernathy would consider her a challenge and wait for her next break to flirt some more and up his game. Or he'd be dancing with another woman by the time her next set started.

She had a feeling it would be the latter. And that was fine with her.

Because Theo Abernathy *definitely* wasn't the guy for her.

Chapter Two

As Theo sat at his table at the wedding—he was friends with both the rodeo-star bride and the rancher groom—he tried to stop staring at the beautiful woman on stage with her band. He'd struck out with Bethany, something he wasn't used to.

"Get her number?" his brother Jace, sitting next to him, asked. "Saw you two chatting it up at the bar."

Theo scowled. "Actually, no. She made an excuse to stop talking to me."

Jace's eyes practically bugged out. He laughed—heartily. "First time?"

Theo actually thought about that. "Yes, it was. I can't help it if I'm the good-looking Abernathy."

Jace's fiancée, Tamara, grinned. "Um, I take issue with that."

Theo laughed. Jace—younger by two years—was engaged and raising one-year-old Frankie, who'd recently had a big first-birthday party, with Tamara. His brother Billy, on the other side of him, the eldest at thirty-eight and the divorced dad of three teenagers, seemed even happier than usual tonight, his fiancée Charlotte beside him. And now Theo's younger sister Robin was engaged too. That was three out of the five Abernathys—all planning weddings. The youngest, Stacy, was the only one besides Theo without a significant other.

Suddenly, Billy lightly clinked his water glass with a spoon, and all eyes at their table turned to him.

"Charlotte and I have an announcement," Billy said. "We told the kids and mom and dad earlier today, so you all are the last to know," he added with a sly smile.

"Know what?" Theo asked, wondering what the big news was.

"We're expecting!" Charlotte said. "I'm pregnant!"

Theo bolted up and pulled his brother and Charlotte into a hug. "I'm gonna be an uncle again! Very happy for you guys."

"The kids are so excited to have a baby sibling," Billy said.

Theo, Jace and Tamara toasted the couple, Billy drinking cranberry juice in solidarity with Charlotte. Theo made a mental note to pick up a gift for them in Hey Baby this week.

He returned his attention to Bethany on stage, and for a few moments he was so mesmerized by that angelic voice, the passion in it, that he barely heard his brother asking him something.

"Don't take it personally, Jace," Tamara said to her fiancé. "Theo's lost to us. He's been *challenged*. And you know how he reacts to a challenge."

Jace laughed. "Oh, yeah. Gives it all he's got until he conquers it."

Thing was, Theo thought, as he took in Bethany Mc-Creery's long, silky, light brown hair, her curvy body so sexy, even in that puffy bridesmaid dress, this wasn't about a challenge. It wasn't about a woman turning down a dance. Or walking away. He'd felt a real connection to Bethany when they'd been talking. Yes, he'd been unable to take his eyes off her, but it was much more than that. He'd rarely felt a connection so quickly.

Which was why when his dates invariably brought up the subject of children, casually mentioning they wanted two or four or *twins*, he made a quick getaway.

He really did want kids—someday. All he knew for sure was that he wasn't ready yet. He loved children—*other* people's. But Theo had lived on his own terms for a long time, and he liked that.

Maybe Bethany was the same. He'd immediately noticed she hadn't been wearing a wedding ring. Single. Like him. And the few times he'd seen her around town, she'd never been with a baby stroller or a kid. Maybe she felt the same way he did about the *not yet*. He tried to remember what she'd said when he mentioned he wasn't ready for children. He drew a blank. Too focused on how pretty she was, her big blue eyes, and that feeling he had when they'd been flirting—when *he'd* been flirting, he realized now.

Hmm. Maybe she just wasn't interested?

Duh, hotshot, she's probably in a serious relationship.

Except she wasn't just the wedding singer at this particular event; she was the groom's sister and a bridesmaid. She surely had been invited with a plus-one. And if she'd come with a date, he would have muscled his way over when Theo had been standing a half inch from her at the bar and clearly going for it.

She just wasn't interested, he thought, which *did* send up challenge signals. Challenges were exciting; his brother and Tamara had that right about him.

Theo would find Bethany after the last song of the night,

when the guests were leaving, and…what? Ask her for her number, which he hadn't even had the chance to do? Yes, he'd start there. If she didn't want to give it to him, he'd take no for an answer. He was a gentleman, after all. The code of the West called for it.

For the first time in Theo Abernathy's life, since he was, say, twelve, he didn't dance a single dance with a woman at a wedding. And he'd been to plenty in the past few years.

As the night went on, Theo tried to stop being so aware of Bethany—on stage or off, when he'd catch her mingling. She danced with her brother, with her parents, with the other bridesmaids. Once he saw a guy he vaguely knew through the ranching community approach her and then walk away after five seconds. *Strikeout*, he thought happily. So it wasn't just him. She wasn't dancing with any man.

He himself had been approached at least ten times by single women during the course of the night, and he had made kind excuses. He didn't want to dance with anyone but Bethany McCreery.

Finally, the wedding was winding down. The band was collecting their instruments. He watched Bethany hug the three guys—guitarist, keyboardist, and drummer—and then come down the stage steps. Her parents hugged her, the bride hugged her, a bunch of other people hugged her.

Finally, she was alone.

It's now or never, he told himself.

He caught her eye as he was heading toward her. Unless he was flattering himself—something he did probably a little too often—she seemed excited to see him. Something in the way her eyes sparkled. But as he stepped up to her, she seemed…wary.

Hmm. Challenge part two: figuring her out.

"I just wanted to say again how much I loved listening to you sing," he said. "You're so talented." Every word was true. Even if he wasn't romantically interested, he'd say all this.

She gave him a warm smile that reached right inside him. "I really appreciate that. Thank you."

"I can't leave without at least trying to get your number," he said. The flirtation had gone out of his voice, he realized. He wanted her number—badly.

She looked away for a second, then started talking really fast about how her life was very complicated right now, a lot going on, booked weekends, some family events.

Wow. She really didn't want to go out with him. Or get to know him better.

Disappointment socked him in the stomach. He wanted to save them both from this uncomfortable moment, so he said, "I, uh, was asking because three of my siblings are engaged and will be getting married in the coming months, and I can pass along your contact info—as a wedding singer."

Her face flushed for a moment. Great. Now he'd made her feel foolish for thinking he was asking her out—when he was.

He sighed. "Full disclosure, Bethany. I asked for your number because I was hoping we could get to know each other. I'd love to take you out to dinner. Or a walk on my ranch—it has some gorgeous spots to watch the sunset over the mountains. I know you said you were taking a break from dating, but you can't blame a guy for trying, right?"

She gave him something of a smile. "I really like your honesty, Theo. That's the second thing you were very open about."

"What was the first?"

"Not wanting children in the near future," she said.

He raised an eyebrow. "You do?" he asked. He didn't know a thing about her, he realized. Maybe she did and *that* was the problem.

"I definitely do," she said.

"Oh" was what stupidly came out of his mouth.

"If you give me your phone," she said, "I'll put in my contact info for you to pass to your siblings. Networking is everything," she added with a kind of fake cheer.

He handed over his phone, and she entered her info, then gave his phone back.

He texted her a Hi so that she'd have his number too.

Not that she'd ever use it.

"Well, bye!" she said and then fled.

He let out a hard sigh. He'd mangled that.

But as he watched her catch up with a couple of other bridesmaids at the door, he was aware of how much he already wanted to see her again.

Bethany was on her way home from the wedding when she found herself passing right by her apartment building and making a right at the next street instead. Her parents' house was a few miles away, and that was where she wanted to be.

She'd come so close to blurting out to Theo that she was pregnant. *Not only do I want children in the near future, but I'll be having a baby in five months!*

But no way would she tell anyone before her mother.

It was late, but the news couldn't wait. Besides, her mom would be awake, too excited to go to bed now that her firstborn was married. She'd be up and in the kitchen, making tea and having a little bit more of the wedding cake the bride and groom had insisted she take home, and looking through the hundreds of photos and videos she'd no doubt taken with her cell phone.

When Bethany pulled into her parents' driveway, the kitchen lights were on.

She texted her mom that she was here. Her mom responded immediately.

Wide-awake and in the kitchen making tea. Come on in.

Ha, called that one, she thought with relief that she could talk to her mom right now. But butterflies let loose in her belly at actually sharing the news. She was the only one who knew her secret since she'd been surprised with the discovery at seven weeks along.

She tapped on the door, and her mom opened it, tears in her blue eyes.

"Aww, emotional?" Bethany said, her own eyes misting.

"My baby got married," Raye McCreery said, opening her arms for a hug. She still wore her lacy, pale pink mother-of-the-groom dress, her ash-brown hair in an elegant updo.

Bethany flew into her mom's arms. Best feeling in the world.

"Dad dozing in the recliner in the living room?" Bethany asked as she sat down at the kitchen table.

"You know it." Her mom poured two cups of herbal tea and set out the big hunk of wedding cake.

"I barely got to try it," Bethany said, digging her fork into a piece. "Yum," she said. "Both rich and light at the same time. Magical."

She really had no appetite. She was just stalling. Bethany looked out the window, the moon almost a perfect crescent.

"You okay?" her mom asked, eyeing her. "Did the wedding bring up some stuff for you?"

Bethany wasn't surprised by the question. She and her mom had always been close, and Bethany had shared her worry that she'd let love pass her by. And had suddenly woken up one day thirty-five and single.

With a serious case of baby fever.

"Well, it did," Bethany said, "but the reason I'm very emotional right now—and have been the past few months— is because of something else."

Her mother paused, fork midway to her mouth. She set it down. "What, honey?"

Bethany bit her lip. *Here goes. The cat out of the ole bag.* "Let me start from the beginning."

Raye nodded and sipped her tea.

"You know I've always enjoyed being single, living the life of a wedding singer, constantly on the road, traveling from wedding to wedding," Bethany said. "And I always believed that eventually, I'd find my Mr. Right and get married. Well, eventually never came, but thirty-five did. My biological clock has been ticking really loudly."

Her mom was listening intently, and Bethany could tell she was forcing herself not to interject or interrupt. Raye McCreery was already a grandmother times three—and now five, counting Elizabeth's twin five-year-old girls— but she was excited for Bethany to add to the brood.

She took a long sip of her tea, the chamomile scent and warmth so comforting. "Back in January," she said, "with the new year, I started exploring my options, particularly single motherhood via a sperm bank and in vitro fertilization."

Her mom's eyes widened, and she quickly ate a bite of cake so she'd stay quiet. Bethany had to smile at how well she knew her mother.

"But in the midst of reading brochures and websites and even visiting a clinic," she continued, "I had a very unexpected…encounter with Rexx Winters. You remember him, right? He used to be the bassist in my band?"

Her mom nodded. "Nice guy. Handsome too. Could use a haircut, in my opinion."

Bethany smiled. Rexx had always been in need of a haircut with that floppy mop of his.

"Well, one night, after a wedding at a ridiculously over-the-top country club in Billings, Rexx and I ended up kissing. We'd both had a little too much champagne. And one kiss led to another and suddenly we were in my hotel room. In the morning, we were both a little embarrassed and agreed it was a onetime thing, that aside from the basic attraction and the band, we had little in common and not much chemistry."

Raye was hanging on her every word, clearly wondering where this was going.

"Well, I was hard on myself afterward," Bethany said, "thinking that was exactly why I was still single at thirty-five. Something brought me and Rexx together, and immediately afterward, there I was saying no, writing it off, not even giving the idea of a relationship with him a chance. So I was thinking about that, and a week later, we performed at another wedding, this one on a lake with such a beautiful setting, and it was so romantic and the ceremony so emotional that I got wistful. I decided I'd talk to Rexx about giving us a try."

"And he said?" her mom prompted.

"Well, I couldn't find him that night. But in the morning, the band met for breakfast, and I pulled him aside after so we could talk, and before I could say anything, he told me he finally understood what all these weddings were about, that he'd fallen head over heels for a bridesmaid last night and knew immediately she was The One and that he'd marry her. After knowing her a few hours!"

"Oh, Bethany, I'm so sorry," her mom said.

Bethany sighed. "Two weeks later, he called a meeting of the band, told us he was engaged and was quitting to follow his fiancée to her home in Colorado. I thought wow, I was really going to try to work at a relationship with a man I don't have feelings for. That's not good. So right then and there, I decided to pursue in vitro fertilization and make my dream of a family—a child—come true."

"Wow!" her mother said. "So you're going ahead with it now?"

"There's more to the story," Bethany said, quickly having another bite of cake. "At my appointment, I was examined by the doctor, and about ten minutes later, the doctor and nurse returned to the exam room to say, 'Surprise, you're *already* pregnant.'"

Her mother gasped.

"Yup, that was my reaction," Bethany said.

"What did Rexx say?" her mom asked.

Bethany sighed. "I debated telling him at all because of the situation with his new love—throwing a monkey wrench into that. But I decided of course I had to tell him. He deserved to know. And the baby deserved the father to know about him or her. But when I called him, he immediately cut me off and said he was engaged and very happy and needed to leave his past in the past. He disconnected the call before I could tell him the big news."

"So he doesn't know?"

Bethany shook her head. "You're the only one who does."

"And me," came a voice from the doorway. Her father stood there, holding out his arms. Mack McCreery was still in his suit, now a bit rumpled like his graying brown hair.

Bethany got up and flew into her dad's embrace. Her mom came over, and they had a family hug.

"We're gonna be grandparents again, Raye!" her dad said excitedly. "Where are my cigars?"

Bethany absolutely loved that that was his takeaway from that whole story. "You two will the best grandparents in the world." Doting, loving, and *there*. She could always count on her parents.

"Doesn't it just figure that both Jake and Elizabeth either sold or gave away all their baby stuff from five kiddos?" her mom said. "I've been to your apartment and know you haven't bought anything for the baby—unless you've been hiding things in the closet."

Bethany shook her head. "The day I found out I was pregnant, it didn't feel quite real. So I went to the baby section of a store outside Bronco where I wouldn't run into anyone I knew and bought two things—adorable yellow fleece pj's, since the baby will be born in November, when it's chilly. And a floppy stuffed rabbit with long ears. But that's it so far."

The pj's were in the dresser in Bethany's spare bedroom. She'd moved to the apartment just last year, when she'd started thinking about her future, about wanting a baby. Her lease had come up for renewal on the tiny one-bedroom she'd lived in for the past decade, and she hadn't been able to bear signing it again—signing up for another year of not moving forward on her dreams. Every now and then, she'd go into the spare room she envisioned as a nursery and look at the bunny sitting on the dresser. She'd open the drawer and take out the yellow pj's and hold them, and she'd feel such hope, that her dream of having a baby would happen.

"You can count on us to help, honey," her dad said. "We'll get what you need before the baby comes. Don't you worry about anything, okay?"

Her eyes did mist up then. "I love you two so much," Bethany said. "I don't know what I'd do without you."

They had another group hug, then sat down at the table. Her dad poured himself a mug of tea and dug into the cake, instantly getting a little chocolate icing on his tie.

"Eh," he said, taking another bite.

Bethany and her mom laughed. She might be facing single motherhood, but she was doing it with the best parents in Montana.

Chapter Three

Coffee thermos in hand, Theo left his cabin on the property of the Bonnie B and walked the half mile to the ranch office to meet his brothers. He breathed in the fresh summer air, the family ranch with its majestic evergreens, the mountains in the distance, and the cattle dotting the pastures and ridges of the ranch never failing to rejuvenate him. The Bonnie B was truly a family affair and not too far from his aunt and uncle's ranch, the Flying A. Except for Theo's youngest sibling, Stacy, a teacher, all the Abernathys worked for the ranch in some capacity. Theo focused on cattle management, but at heart he was a cowboy.

He let out a yawn, which was unlike him. Theo usually slept like a rock. Not last night. He'd been unable to stop thinking about Bethany McCreery. Or her voice.

His grandmother had had a favorite phrase, and it came to him right then: *Don't court trouble.*

He'd be doing just that by pursuing Bethany. He could see it now—they'd be dating three months, getting serious, and she'd bring up the subject of starting a family. At thirty-five, her biological clock had to be a major factor in the timeline. He understood that.

But a first baby at *forty* sounded right to Theo. Maybe even forty-two.

When you knew you had different wants, different goals *before* the first date, there shouldn't *be* a first date.

That was Basic Life Skills 101. And because he *was* thirty-five, Theo should know better.

Don't court trouble...

Except he couldn't stop thinking about her. Dang it.

He drank some coffee, waved at the two cowboys on horseback who were heading past him out into the far pastures, and tried to focus on this morning's meeting. Usually, Theo and his brothers didn't schedule meetings on Saturdays, let alone after a wedding that had kept them out late. But they all had packed schedules, particularly with family commitments, so this morning was the only time they could get together to talk about the upcoming cattle auctions.

In the office, which was attached to the main house where his parents lived, he found his brothers at the coffee station. The three Abernathys looked alike, as everyone said, tall with green eyes.

"Third cup," Jace said, holding up his mug. "And it's only 9:00 a.m." He took a sip and then sat down on his desk chair, facing out. "Frankie's teething and woke up a couple times, including just past 3:00 a.m."

Theo didn't know how his brother was standing. Back when just-turned-a-year-old Frankie woke multiple times a night, there was Jace with the baby bottle, rubbing the boy's little back, or walking the house with him to soothe his cries. Theo knew this because his fiancée, Tamara, often talked about what a great dad Jace was.

How was his younger brother so ready to be a dad when Theo wasn't? Then again, Frankie had come into Jace's life as a foster baby. A volunteer firefighter, Jace had rescued the baby's pregnant mother from a house fire and delivered the child before the mother unfortunately died of smoke inhalation. Distraught at the experience, Jace had surprised everyone—himself included—by insisting on taking responsibility for the infant. Tamara, an ER nurse, had helped him care for Frankie, and they'd started forming a family without even realizing it.

"Second for me," Billy said, refilling his own mug. "I've got a busy day." He glanced at his phone, which was balanced on his knee. "And about fifteen minutes before I need to drop off all three teens at different places. I veer between dreaming of them getting their driver's licenses and realizing Charlotte and I will actually have to *teach* them to drive. Sitting in the passenger seat without a foot on the brake? No, thanks."

Jace laughed. "Yeah, I'm glad I've got a good fifteen years till permit time." He pulled up the cattle auction website on his desktop. The three of them had already made their decisions on the additions for the ranch; it was more a matter of timing. The auctions would be ongoing for three days but were a good forty-five minutes away from Bronco. It was looking like the three of them would need to attend separately.

Jace eyed the screen and shook his head as he relayed the days and times for the auctions. "Monday's not good for me. I take care of Frankie solo on Monday. I can go to the Tuesday auction."

"That works, since Tuesday's out for me," Billy said. "I'm volunteering as a camp chaperone for a hiking expedition. I can go Wednesday morning."

"Not for me," Jace said. "Frankie has a well-baby checkup that morning."

MELISSA SENATE   33

Just the usual meeting among the brothers. Trying to plan anything when Jace and Billy had such busy lives was often impossible.

"I'll take the other day," Theo said. "My only responsibility is the ranch."

"I can't even remember when that was my life," Billy said with a smile.

Jace nodded and sipped his coffee. "*I* can barely remember, and it's only been a year since I became a dad."

Case in point, Theo thought. He could attend a cattle auction any day of the week he damn well pleased.

"Okay, now that that's settled," Billy said, taking a sip of his coffee, "let's move to very important matters—like your love life, Theo. Did you get Bethany's number last night?"

Wasn't he trying not to think about the beautiful wedding singer?

Especially after this? The woman wanted kids right away. She'd said so.

"Actually, I did," Theo said, dropping down in a chair across from the desks. "But I don't know if we want the same things right now."

Billy raised an eyebrow. "You could tell that after talking for, like, all of fifteen minutes during her break?"

Well, yeah. Because he'd been up front. And she'd been up front.

"Go on a date," Jace said. "Then decide."

That was a problem. He barely knew Bethany Mc-Creery and couldn't manage to get her off his mind. Two, three hours on a date, just them, sitting across from each other at a romantic restaurant, and he'd be a goner.

He knew it.

And then what? He was nowhere near ready for kids. She was.

So why start something?

Just then Tamara came in holding baby Frankie, her son's little fist wrapped around a hank of Tamara's long brown hair. Theo watched Jace's eyes light up at the sight of both of them. His brother bolted up to give his fiancée a kiss, and Theo didn't miss the passion in the three-second kiss on the lips, the tenderness in Jace's gaze as he looked at the baby, cupped his little cheek.

I can't see it for me, Theo thought, sipping his coffee.

He got up to greet Tamara and to play a round of peek-aboo with his nephew. Frankie's big eyes locked on Theo as he moved his hands away his face with a "Peekaboo! I see you!"

The baby laughed, the sound going right into Theo's heart. Both his brothers often said there was no greater sound on earth than a baby's laughter. Theo had to agree.

"Hold him for a second?" Tamara asked Theo. "I need to get all this hair into a ponytail. You'd think I'd have learned to do that before I carry Frankie anywhere, but nope." She laughed. "Theo, try to free me from the iron grip, will ya?"

Theo laughed too and gave Frankie's tummy a tickle. The baby let go of his mom's hair.

"Ah," she said, handing the baby over to Theo.

He held Frankie out and studied him. "Good grip, little man," he said. "That's the way you'll be holding the reins in a few years when you get on your first pony."

"Hey, maybe he'll take after me and go into the medical field," Tamara said. She smiled and shook her head. "Eh, who am I kidding? He'll be a rancher like most Abernathys."

Theo cuddled his baby nephew against him and gave him a gentle pat on his back.

Which was when a big glop of baby spit-up landed on his favorite faded denim shirt.

Jace and Billy burst out laughing.

"Good aim, Frankie ole boy," Jace said when he recovered from his laughing fit.

"Yeah, you chose well, kiddo," Billy added. "Better Uncle Theo than me."

Theo mock narrowed his eyes at his adorable nephew. "You can spit up on me anytime, Frankie."

Because I get to give you back. Getting thrown up on was a novelty.

"Well, *I'm* sorry," Tamara said with a smile, her hair now safely in a ponytail. "Here, I'll take him."

Theo happily handed over the drooler.

Maybe he *wouldn't* call Bethany.

As a wedding singer, Bethany always held meetings with potential clients in their homes, because they invariably wanted to hear a live a cappella performance, and she couldn't belt out Celine Dion or Frank Sinatra or the bride-to-be's favorite song in the middle of the Gemstone Diner or Kendra's Cupcakes. On Saturday morning at ten, Bethany sat in the kind of living room she'd only seen in very fancy home decor magazines and websites devoted to interior design. The sofas were white and pristine and looked like they'd been delivered that morning. Bethany didn't yet have a child or a pet, and she'd *still* had to turn over the cushions on her nubby textured sofa from a thrift store because of a juice spill when she'd been spooked during a thunderstorm.

Sitting across from Bethany was Laurene Fields, a bride-to-be whose wedding Bethany *had* to secure because she needed the deposit to allow her to take a solid three months for maternity leave. Laurene had already said she'd double the band's usual fee because she was getting married on Valentine's Day night.

Like I'd have a date to cancel because of work. No problem there.

Laurene and her fiancé were both mega wealthy and were having a "sky's the limit" wedding. Bethany knew this because Laurene had told her so—at least three times since she'd arrived at Laurene's huge house in Bronco Heights. Bethany used to occasionally babysit Laurene, who was seven years younger, but Laurene claimed not to remember her. Bethany and her band were on Laurene's radar because they'd performed at her cousin's wedding and had apparently made quite an impression on Laurene. That was one of the perks of being part of a wedding band—so many potential clients among the guests.

Laurene had gotten engaged only last night and had called Bethany early this morning for the meeting. *I'm hoping you can meet before noon*, Laurene had said. *I have a million calls to make.* Bethany had dropped everything to squeeze it in—she had an afternoon wedding to get ready for and would have liked to just spend the morning resting since she got tired easily these days, like now.

But she would not let one yawn escape her while with Laurene.

Her other plans for the morning had involved coming up with ways to get Theo Abernathy off her mind. Nothing worked. She'd woken up thinking about him, and had tried to keep their conversation about children on a running loop.

Her: *You don't want kids?*

Him: *I'm sure I do,* someday. *But I just don't feel ready yet. That's a lot of responsibility, a lot of sacrifice.*

His face kept creeping into her thoughts. His long, muscular body. And the past month, she'd thought she'd lost her sex drive. Turned out she was wrong.

She'd tried telling herself that he had a new girlfriend every week. She didn't know if that was even true, but it probably was. Then again, he hadn't gone to Jake and Elizabeth's wedding with a date. Interesting. Or maybe not. Maybe weddings were among his favorite places to meet someone.

He had met someone. Her. It just hadn't gone anywhere—and couldn't.

"Can you sing the first few lines of these songs?" Laurene asked, handing her a list and breaking into her renegade thoughts.

Bethany took the piece of paper and smiled. All classic wedding songs.

Bethany sang away, and Laurene surprised her by holding a hand over her heart.

"I just love your voice," Laurene gushed. "You sound like you mean it."

Bethany smiled. Yes! This gig just might be hers and the band's. They could all use double their usual fee. They'd get half up front, half on the wedding day. "I appreciate that."

"I can tell you right now that you're hired," Laurene

said. "I knew at my cousin Tara's wedding that when I got married, I'd have to have you as the singer. My fiancé, CJ, agreed—he was my plus-one."

"Count on us, then," Bethany said, relief flooding her. She could take off those three months and not rely on her parents so much for babysitting—particularly for weddings that ran till well after midnight.

"I'm so excited to be engaged!" Laurene trilled, holding out her engagement ring. "The proposal was everything! He hired a skywriter to propose over our picnic spot at my family's ranch."

"That's so romantic," Bethany said and could hear the wistful edge in her voice.

"Our wedding will be on Valentine's Day, and we'll have our first baby by Christmas. Then our second, third and fourth every three years thereafter. Of course, I'm hoping for twins—they do run in our family." She slid a glance at Bethany's left hand. At her blank ring finger. "Not married?" she asked, surprise in her expression.

"No," Bethany said, biting her lip. "Just haven't found my Mr. Right."

"And no children, then?" Laurene continued. "Wow, aren't you like *thirty-five*?"

Bethany wanted to say, *Well, I* am *pregnant*, but she was sure she'd only gets look of pity at having to be a single mother. And no doubt Laurene would say something like *Maybe you'll meet someone at my wedding*.

Bethany's phone vibrated. She glanced at it on the coffee table. Theo Abernathy's name popped up on the screen.

Her heart lifted. She needed to feel like she had a prospect in that moment.

Wait a minute. Theo was *not* a prospect.

She certainly couldn't answer the call during a work meeting, especially when Laurene was going on and on about how much CJ loved her.

Just when Bethany was bursting with envy over the bride-to-be's stories of how sweet her fiancé was, Laurene's phone rang with a hopeful caterer needing to meet earlier, so she had to run.

Outside the swanky apartment complex with its indoor and outdoor pools and a view of the mountains, Bethany texted her bandmates that the gig was theirs. They all sent back dollar and heart emojis.

It wasn't until Bethany was in her car that she realized her baby would be a few months old on Valentine's and that she'd want to celebrate the coming new year as a mother with her baby. She'd be going back to work early.

Bethany was used to a life of compromise and making things work. The money would be worth it.

She tapped her phone icon for recent calls. There was Theo's name. He'd left a voice mail.

She hit Play.

Hi, Bethany, it's Theo. First of all, I don't want you think I'm bad at listening. I heard what you said about taking a break from dating, but... The thing is, we had a connection and that's unusual for me, so... Okay, how about this. Call me back if you don't think it's a really bad idea.

Bethany had to smile. It *was* a bad idea, and they both knew it.

But he was feeling the same way she was.

Because of that connection he'd mentioned. And how

rare was that? For Bethany, *very*. She thought of all the dates she'd had in the six months before she'd decided to look into single motherhood. She'd gone out with all kinds of men. From fix ups to a dating app to a few guys she'd happened to meet while simply being out and about in town. She'd start out excited about possibilities and end up just feeling lonely.

All right, here's what you do, she thought. *You go out with Theo Abernathy. Since it's a date, you'll both see really fast that of course it can't go anywhere. You'll both have gotten the what-if out of your systems. Then maybe you can be friends.*

She called him back.

The moment she heard his voice, she felt happy butterflies flutter in her belly.

"I called back to tell you we *should* go out so that we'd see for ourselves it's a bad idea. We'll both run for the hills after a half hour."

He laughed. "I'll wear my sneakers, then. How about tonight?"

Tonight? That was coming right up. She suddenly felt nervous, those butterflies flapping hard. "Hmm, tonight's not good for me." Going out with him at all was asking for trouble. This man had her all turned around.

"Tomorrow night?" he asked.

She bit her lip. "Tomorrow's not good either."

"Any day next week, then," he said.

I'm busy for the next eighteen years, she wanted to say.

"My life is actually pretty complicated right now," she said. "In fact, we should just forget going out." Yes, they should. Spending a few hours in his company would only make her crave him *more*. Not less.

"I can't," he said. "To be very honest. I'd like to get to know you better. That's what I know for absolute sure. Tell you what—how about if we just get together, a walk on the Bonnie B? I'll show you my favorite spot to watch the sunset. My favorite goat. My favorite of the spring calves."

"Monday," she blurted out before she could not say it. "I don't have a wedding on Monday, so I'm free."

"Monday, July first," Theo said. "I'm penning it in."

She laughed. "It's a date." Her smile faded very fast. "I mean, it's… We're getting together."

Now he laughed. "It's okay, Bethany. It's a *walk*."

But it wasn't just *a walk*. It was the start of something. And she knew it.

Chapter Four

"And that's Buster, our new rooster," Theo said late Monday afternoon, pointing at the golden comet strutting around the chicken barn on his family's ranch.

Bethany wasn't surprised that the chickens—and Buster—had more than just a coop. The Bonnie B had many beautiful outbuildings, from ornate stables for the horses to stately red barns of various sizes for the cattle and equipment. What Theo referred to as bunkhouses for the employees who lived on the ranch were more like luxe cabins, and what he called cabins, like what he and his siblings lived in on the huge, majestic property, were log *mansions*.

"Love the name Buster," she said. "Did you name him?"

"My teenaged nephew got naming rights for the newest rooster, and we were all a little nervous at what he'd come up with. We can barely understand half his slang these days. But he declared him Buster, and we all love it too."

She liked that Theo talked a lot about his family, and not just his parents and siblings and their significant others but his aunts and uncles and cousins. It was clear the Abernathys were a tight-knit group, just like the McCreerys, and there were *a lot* of Abernathys in town.

She liked him, period, she thought as she bent down to pet a fluffy reddish-brown chicken pecking the ground near her feet. Theo was such a gentleman. He'd picked her up exactly on time for their "just a walk," had come upstairs to her second-floor landing when she'd buzzed him in, then held open the passenger door of his shiny pickup for her and closed it when she was settled inside. She wasn't used to that.

And maybe it was the wealth, but for a man in jeans and a Western shirt and cowboy boots, he managed to look *dressed*. She'd poked around her closet for just the right flowy sundress, then realized she shouldn't try to hide her baby bump anymore. Especially now that she'd told her parents. This might not be a *date* date, but it sure felt like one, and she'd have to tell Theo she was expecting at some point during this get-together. Maybe even early on.

Like now.

Blurting it out here, out of the clear blue, didn't seem like the time or the place, though. It would sound as though she'd been holding it in, holding it back, which was exactly what she was doing. Would he say, *Why the heck did you agree to go out with me, then?*

Probably. She hadn't told him at the wedding because she'd wanted to tell her mom first. And she hadn't told him when they'd spoken on the phone because...

She didn't have a good answer for that.

She'd had the past hour to tell him. And there'd been a time or two when she could have brought it up as they'd walked around the Bonnie B. Their conversation had centered mostly on their families, the two of them swapping sweet, funny stories about their nieces and nephews. But just as she'd been about to bring up the subject of her own child-to-be, he'd pointed out something on the ranch— the spot where he liked to watch the sunset and how if he needed to clear his head, he'd just walk the land, keeping his gaze focused on the cattle on the ridges in the distance, the green pastures as far as she could see, the mountains.

They'd talked easily, an hour passing in a snap. And the entire time she'd rationalized her interest in him to how nice it would be to have Theo Abernathy as a *friend*.

A friend who happened to be very good-looking and deliciously built. She was well aware that she didn't notice every little detail about her male friends—like the mesmerizing green of Theo's eyes or the way the sunlight spun gold into his brown hair. He had a habit of running a hand through that hair when he was thinking about an answer to something she'd asked.

She wasn't going to kid herself about Theo. She was very attracted to him—the man who didn't want children anytime soon.

But she wasn't ready to say goodbye.

And not because she hadn't told him her big news. She gave the chicken one last pat, then stood. Maybe she would just blurt it out right now.

"I like a woman who isn't afraid to get close to a chicken," he said. "Not too long ago, one of my sisters set me up on a blind date with a friend of hers who grew up on a ranch but hated it her whole life. You'd think Stacy would have figured that would never work."

Bethany laughed. "My last blind date told me he couldn't stand live music—'it's so loud and all those annoying people singing along'—and that he hated that his dates were always suggesting going to concerts and music festivals. I said, 'Um, you know I'm a wedding singer, right? Live music is what I do.'" She shook her head. "That pretty much sums up how my dates went before—"

She clammed up. She'd been about to say: before she gave up on men and decided on in vitro fertilization, only to discover—surprise!—that she'd gotten pregnant the old-fashioned way.

That was a story in itself. And one she couldn't imagine telling Theo just like that.

"Before?" he prompted, glancing at her.

She bit her lip. He'd been doing this since he'd picked her up. Listening. Asking questions.

Making her like him. Dangerous when she was already so attracted. And had raging hormones.

"Before I took a break from dating," she said fast.

"Miss it?" he asked.

She laughed again. "Miss dating? Are you kidding?"

"Yeah, really dumb question," he said with a smile that sent goose bumps along the nape of her neck. "Except this kind of redeems the whole dating process," he added, wagging a finger between them.

Her heart lifted at the sweetness of what he'd just said, then crashed. Sigh. Wasn't it always like this? Right man, wrong time. Right time, wrong man. "This isn't really a date, though," she reminded him. "It's a *walk*."

He laughed, and she wanted to reach for his hand and just hold it. Why did she have to feel so close to this man?

"I suddenly have a mad craving for pasta," Theo said as they watched the rooster strut around. "Linguine carbonara with garlic bread. Hungry?"

Uh-oh. That would make this more than a walk. Dinner meant *date*. But now that he'd mentioned pasta and garlic bread, she had a major craving for both herself. And once a craving hit, there was no ignoring it. "Ooh, me too. But for penne primavera in a pink cream sauce. And definitely the garlic bread."

"Pastabilities?" he asked.

The casual Italian restaurant in Bronco Heights was perfect for tonight—not too romantic, not too date-like. Just right.

"I love that place," she said, her craving for garlic bread so strong now she just might order it as an appetizer.

He smiled. "Great. Off we go."

If he'd suggested riding there together on a white horse, she wouldn't have been surprised. He'd been having a knight-in-shining-armor effect on her this whole time. Which made absolutely no sense. Once she told Theo Abernathy she was pregnant—and she would before the night was over—he'd run for those hills. She'd never see him again.

They got back into the shiny pickup that probably cost the equivalent of three years' rent on her apartment. Twenty minutes later, they were seated at a table for two in Pastabilities by a window facing the main street and handed menus, the waiter asking about their drink orders. Theo opted for a hard lemonade. She said she'd have the soft version.

She waited for a light bulb to magically go off over his head like in cartoons. *Oh, you're not drinking, therefore you must be pregnant!*

No such luck.

When he mentioned that he might start with a Caesar salad, she could have said she loved rich, creamy Caesar dressing—and she actually had a serious craving for croutons and shaved Parmesan now—but raw egg yolk was a no-no on the pregnancy diet.

Instead she said she wanted to save her appetite for the main course.

"Hey, look," Theo said, upping his chin toward the window. "There goes your new sister-in-law's family."

Bethany looked where he was gesturing and smiled. It was no surprise he knew who they were. Three of Elizabeth's sisters, very popular rodeo stars who performed together as the Hawkins Sisters, were deep in conversation as they walked across the street.

Bethany turned her attention back to Theo, who was sipping his drink. "Jake and Elizabeth and the kids are on their familymoon. They're spending the week together right here in Bronco."

"I like that. Big blended family, right?"

She chuckled and nodded. "Five kids—Elizabeth's twin five-year-olds, Lucy and Gianna, and Jake's three—ten-year-old Molly, eight-year-old Peter, and six-year-old Ben."

"Wow, that's *a lot* of young children," Theo said. "I can't imagine coordinating that. My brother Billy has three teenagers, and just getting them to their summer activities takes incredible feats of timing between him and Charlotte. Plus, they just announced to the family that they're expecting a baby in January."

She felt her eyes widen. There was her in. *Me too—but in November!* she could say. But that wasn't what came out of her mouth. "Ah yes, that unmagical time of constant plans and no driver's licenses yet. I remember that from when Jake and I were teens." She smiled and sipped her lemonade. She just wasn't ready to tell him. For everything to change between them. "Jake and Elizabeth will make it work, though."

"I guess their lives will revolve around the kids," Theo

said. He let out a low whistle to clearly highlight that it sounded like a lot.

Bethany shook her head. "I wouldn't say that. Next week, Elizabeth is performing in the rodeo here in town with the Hawkins Sisters. She doesn't have to give that up. And Jake has his ranch and volunteers at the Pony Club that Elizabeth is heading up—a riding academy for kids. But yes, to a point, they're now accommodating five kids' schedules—but in *addition* to their own."

The waiter came with a tray bearing their orders. The garlic bread smelled heavenly.

"Bon appétit," Bethany said, putting a piece of the bread on her plate.

"Bon appétit," he seconded, twirling his fork in his linguine carbonara.

They dug in for a few minutes, each pronouncing their dishes delicious.

"Try some?" he asked, pushing his bowl toward her.

Of course he was a sharer. Last year she'd gone on a blind date with a cowboy who'd hoarded his truffle fries and not only didn't share but had actually said no when she asked to try one. Deal-breaker right there.

"Mmm, definitely," she said, slipping her fork in. "Ahh. So good." She did the same with her bowl, and he took a forkful of her penne primavera.

"Excellent," he said. "I've loved everything I'd tried here."

"Me too." She picked up her garlic bread and took a very satisfying bite. Ahh, scrumptious.

"Beat you to the table!" came a loud voice.

"No, you won't!" came a louder voice.

Bethany glanced over—identical twins, seven or eight

years old, were racing to a nearby table, their parents, whom she recognized from around town, hurrying over to them.

"We use inside voices in a restaurant," the mom said.

"And we don't run," the dad added.

They sounded more weary than stern. It had likely been a *long* day.

The kids declared that whoever sat down last was a rotten egg. Both boys practically flew to their seats.

The parents sighed and looked around with embarrassed, apologetic expressions.

I can't wait to be you, Bethany thought, smiling at the family. That was life. Busy, harried, beautiful life.

She suddenly wondered if her baby would have a sibling—someday, of course. She knew she wasn't having twins. But maybe in a couple of years...

Getting a little ahead of yourself, Bethany, she thought happily.

"Where are my earplugs?" Theo asked on a laugh. He sent a smile toward the family.

But he probably wasn't kidding.

"Speaking of kids," he said on a chuckle, "I guess I'm used to living life on my own terms. If I had kids, the time and attention I give to the ranch would have to change. I take my responsibilities very seriously, and as a Dad, my kids would come first. Besides, I'd be up at the crack of dawn making a lot of pancakes and probably burning them because I'd be distracted by sibling arguments. And that's after a few years of waking up all night with a crying baby." He gave a mock shiver.

His tone was light, his green eyes twinkling, but Bethany could see he'd *meant* that shiver.

She swallowed. She had to tell him *now*. He was certainly entitled to his point of view. But if he knew she was pregnant, he wouldn't be saying any of this. And that was unfair to him—putting him in a position to feel funny once he did know.

But of course, they wouldn't *be* here at all. Shouldn't be.

She sighed inwardly and glanced out the window. Bethany noticed Bronco's mayor, Rafferty Smith, and his wife, Penny, heading down the street, hand in hand. They'd celebrated their thirtieth anniversary a few months ago. As the couple passed by, Bethany could see Penny was wearing the beautiful antique pearl necklace Rafferty had given her for the occasion.

Thirty years. Back when Bethany used to assume she'd get married "someday," she'd imagined herself growing old with her beloved, sitting on her porch swing, her head on her husband's shoulder, grandchildren playing in the leaves. But here she was, pregnant and on a nondate at age thirty-five—with a man who liked it quiet at 3:00 a.m. because he'd have to wake up with the roosters to start his work day on the ranch.

Hey, just because Theo won't be sitting with you on that porch swing doesn't mean you'll be sitting there alone. You can still find love. Who says you won't be married and celebrating your thirtieth anniversary when you're in your late sixties?

Your brother found love again with three kids.

Elizabeth with two. And twins at that.

She perked up a bit at the thought.

But as she looked at her handsome date, the first man she'd felt a spark within a long time, she wished it *could* be him beside her on the swing.

"But I guess you're ready for your life to dramatically

change," Theo said with a warm smile. "I didn't mean to knock family life. I know you said you're looking forward to that in your near future. It's just not for me right now."

"Well, my future has actually arrived," she said. "I have something to tell you before another second passes. Something I should have told you on the phone when we were making plans."

He was staring at her, head slightly tilted.

Bethany took in a breath. "I'm four months pregnant."

Theo waited a bit just in case she was about to say, *Kidding!*

And waited.

But she didn't say anything else. And she didn't look like she was joking.

"Congratulations," he said somewhat tentatively. He had no idea what her situation was.

Clearly, she wasn't involved with her baby's father if she was here with him, "just a walk" or not.

"I should have told you before tonight that I was pregnant. But when we were talking at my brother's wedding, I hadn't even told my parents. Not to mention the baby's father."

Interesting. There was definitely a story here. "I completely understand," Theo said. "I'm the one who kept trying to talk to you, trying to get your number, trying to make tonight happen. And that's after you told me you wanted a child in the near future."

All true. And he knew why. It had started with her voice; she'd captivated him. And then they'd talked so easily, something very clearly there between them.

If a woman told Theo Abernathy that she wanted a baby now and he'd actually pursued her…

What did that mean?

He didn't have an answer for that one. He hadn't changed his mind about how he felt about being a father now.

They'd both been honest about what they wanted. And they were here because they'd *both* felt that spark.

A little too powerful to ignore.

"And *I'll* completely understand when you get up and leave," she said.

"I'd never do that." He paused, then asked the burning question. The immediate one, anyway. "The father—he's not…"

"In the picture?" she finished for him. "No."

He waited for her to elaborate, but she didn't.

"What are your plans?" he asked. "For when the baby comes?"

She took a long sip of her lemonade. "I'm working as much as I can now to allow me to take maternity leave starting in November. My parents both work, so I'll need to find a nanny or day care. But my plan is to be a great mom."

"I'm sure you will be, Bethany," he said, and he believed she would be despite barely knowing her.

He wanted to know the story. Who the father was. What had happened between them. But he didn't feel he had the right to ask such personal questions.

Besides, after dinner, that would be that for him and Bethany. Right? They didn't know each other. Now was the time to walk away. When they were just two people who'd met at the wrong time.

She'd have a baby in five months.

He couldn't even *imagine* a baby in his life. If he wanted

to record his intro to *This Ranching Life* and edit an episode at 3:00 a.m.—and sometimes he did—he couldn't if
he had a diaper to change or a newborn to feed. He'd be too
bleary-eyed and exhausted and busy to work his side gig,
wouldn't he? And he'd never be able to get through a full
day on the ranch.

No responsibilities except to the Bonnie B and his
family—his two great loves.

Plus, traveling on a moment's notice.

Going out every night—not that he did much of that
anymore. Last Saturday night he'd gone to a family birthday party and was on the couch watching a Marvel movie
at 9:00 p.m. Asleep by midnight. But he *could* be at a
late-night party at the Association or wining and dining
a lovely woman in Vegas for the weekend if he chose to.
In a couple of weeks, he'd be attending eightysomething-
year-old Stanley Sanchez's bachelor party. If he had a
baby, he'd *want* to be home. His life would be so different, and he liked it just the way it was.

"I can see the montage happening in your head," she
said with a smile. "A screaming newborn, a pile of diapers
and burp cloths, baby bottles to wash."

Bachelor parties to leave early.

Huh. Maybe she *did* know him.

Theo Abernathy was rarely speechless. But right now,
he didn't want to say anything.

Anything *final*, he realized, which confused the heck
out of him.

He looked at Bethany, the beautiful singer with the
voice of an angel. The woman he felt this inexplicable connection to. When was the last time he'd talked so easily to
someone he'd just met? Thinking back to her brother and

Elizabeth's wedding, Theo couldn't stop recalling the way he couldn't take his eyes off her, how he didn't want to stop talking to her, how he wanted to get to know her better.

Yeah, he had it bad for this woman. He could hear Billy and Jace insisting that, one day, he too would meet someone and life as he knew it would change. He'd thought they were being dramatic, but here he sat, when the former Theo Abernathy would never have pursued a woman who'd said she wanted a baby soon.

That meant something in itself—and he didn't want to think about it.

"Theo, since you look kind of…ill," she said gently, "let's just call it a night, okay?"

He should be jumping up and running out the door. But he couldn't move. He didn't want to move.

She was studying him, he realized. Trying to figure out why he wasn't getting up.

"Friends?" she said—but then she bit her lip. As if she thought that was a bad idea.

Because of the chemistry. The attraction.

The waiter came over then to ask if they wanted dessert. Bethany said she'd love to have her leftovers wrapped up, including all the garlic bread.

"Pregnancy craving," she added with a sweet smile when the server left.

Oh, God, he thought. He wasn't ready for pregnancy cravings. For something, *anything* taking over. Right now it was cravings and soon it would be exhaustion and then it would be the baby. He couldn't date this woman.

"It's all yours," he said, gesturing to the garlic bread and trying to force a pleasant expression on his face.

But he knew he must look as ill as she'd said.

The waiter returned with her takeout box and the bill. She offered to pay for dinner, but he handed over his credit card and insisted it was his treat.

She thanked him and stood, so he did too.

Just like that, their nondate was over. Before it had ever really had a chance to begin.

They went outside, and it was such a beautiful summer night that, for a moment, he wanted to suggest extending their evening for a stroll around town.

He was in shock. That had to be it.

This never was a date. And they needed to go their separate ways.

Except she'd put friendship on the table.

He drove her home to Bronco Valley in silence, neither of them saying a word until he walked her to her apartment building door.

"Thanks for dinner, Theo. I'll be having the garlic bread for dessert." She smiled, and he knew she was trying to lighten the tension in the air.

He felt like such a heel. He had to say something. But what? What was there to say?

"You're very welcome" was what came out of his mouth.

She gave him another brief smile and quickly unlocked the door and hurried inside.

Leaving him alone with thoughts he didn't know how to process.

Chapter Five

Theo had spent the morning riding fence far out on the ranch, taking photos and notes about repairs that needed to be made. It was someone else's job, a new hire, so Theo rationalized that he was just checking up so he could give the guy feedback. He'd spent most of the afternoon reorganizing the equipment barn, also not his job, and was now in the cattle barn, examining the muck rakes in the locker.

He'd been antsy and unable to focus since he'd woken up that morning, pouring salt instead of sugar into his coffee, looping his belt in his jeans in the wrong direction, Jace had raised an eyebrow and asked him if he'd had enough coffee yet.

Try two refills of his thermos. The caffeine boost hadn't helped.

It was now almost 3:00 p.m., and he still couldn't concentrate, couldn't think straight. Probably because he'd been trying so hard to get Bethany McCreery out of his head. Her face, her voice, her blue eyes, snippets of conversations they'd had—including the major revelation—kept sneaking into his thoughts.

He'd been unsettled since he'd driven Bethany home last night. He hadn't been able to shake it. Not through driving around Bronco Valley or Bronco Heights or walking the ranch in the moonlight.

Why couldn't he just say goodbye? They were wrong for each other. In a life-changing way. And Theo couldn't change his life. He wasn't ready to be a father. And Bethany would have a baby in five months.

What the hell was he going to do? He couldn't imagine just walking away. But how could he not?

Theo sighed hard and tried to focus on the muck rakes hanging in the locker at the end of the line of stalls, checking the wood handles for signs of splintering. Two could use replacing. He jotted that down in his phone's Notes app.

"You gonna start cooking in the caf next?"

Theo turned around to find Jace staring at him from the doorway with a quizzical expression. Billy was beside him, on one knee to pet the family dog and mascot, Bandit. Theo had been so lost in thought he hadn't heard any of them coming. And Bandit usually liked to announce his arrival with a *woof.* That was how far gone Theo was.

Billy grinned. "Please say no, Theo. Whatever has you doing every job on the Bonnie B but your own, please keep out of the caf's kitchen. You can barely flip a burger before it burns on one side. The cowboys and cowgirls and hands will revolt."

Both his brothers chuckled at how true that was, then they sobered up, continuing their deep study of him.

"Okay, what's going on with you?" Billy asked.

"Something is definitely up," Jace added.

Theo was about to say he was fine. That nothing was up at all. But just then, a memory overtook him—of beautiful Bethany in her flowered sundress telling him that not only was she four months pregnant but that the father wasn't in the picture.

He sucked in a breath and told his brothers everything— swearing them to secrecy since this was Bethany's private business. He needed their take on the situation. They were both engaged, they were both dads, and both had worked very hard to get where they were today: happy family men. Plus, they knew him very well.

"Here's what I think," Jace said. "Being friends with Bethany means dating without the sex for maybe the first week. You'll call yourselves friends, but mutual attraction won't go away. Trust me, you'll be in a romantic relationship by week's end."

Billy shook his head. "I don't know about that. I think the two of you will *repel* each other. Theo, you're not gonna be attracted to a woman who'll have a baby in five months, because a baby is not what you want. And she won't be attracted to a man who isn't interested in parenthood right now. So the attraction *will* disappear and you can be friends."

"If that were the case," Jace said, "he wouldn't be in this quandary. She told him flat out she wanted a baby soon, but he pursued her, anyway. And he told her flat out that he doesn't want to be a dad for, like, five years, but she said yes to the date. Oh, excuse me—a *walk*." He smiled and shook his head. "The two of you are a lost cause, sorry."

"Hmm," Billy said, considering that. "Kid brother might be right here, Theo. Sorry. You two will shake on friendship, but in a week or two, you'll be seriously dating a pregnant woman. Just know that from the outset."

Jace laughed. "Yup. I mean, look at *us*. Not quite the same situation, but…"

Theo did look at his two brothers, and his head almost exploded. The idea of being a father hadn't been a thought in Jace's head when he'd found himself taking in the orphaned newborn he'd delivered. But his brother had been unable to walk away from Frankie. And despite not looking for love herself, the ER nurse who'd examined the baby was now his fiancée.

Then there was Billy. Engaged to the very woman who'd stood him up at his own wedding twenty years earlier. The recently divorced dad of three teenagers had been dealing with betrayal and custody questions—and was now actually excited about planning his wedding to Charlotte Taylor. They were expecting a baby in January, and Theo knew how excited his brother was about the new addition to the family. *Four* kids!

He swallowed. Surely Theo had a say in all this. It was, after all, his life. "Maybe I'd better keep my distance from her."

"Until the baby's born, anyway," Jace said. "Once you see her with a squawking baby crying his little heart out in Bronco Java and Juice when you just want a strawberry-banana smoothie, you'll be fine. You can be friends then."

Theo caught the sly smile that passed between his older and younger brothers.

"Ha, just kidding," Jace added. "The problem with someone getting under your skin is that you won't be able to stay away. You'll be bringing her dinner tonight, no doubt. All the foods she's craving, like pickled herring and pickled eggs."

Billy grimaced. "I think you're confusing *pickled* with *pickles*. Pickles are the standard craving for pregnant women."

Theo had no idea what pickled herring was—or pickled eggs, for that matter. "So what you're both saying loud and clear is that I shouldn't even bother thinking about this life crisis because it's out of my hands."

"Pretty much," Jace said. "This thing," he added, slapping a hand over his heart, "will be directing you from now."

"But, very seriously, Theo," Billy said. "You can't casually date a pregnant woman. You're either in it or you're not."

Theo let out a hard sigh.

What Billy had just said was exactly the problem. There was no casual when it came to pregnancy. To a baby coming in five months. To a woman who was a package deal.

Theo *couldn't* be in it. "I know I'm not ready to be a dad," he said. "I'm meant to be fun Uncle Theo. Giving kids *back* after two hours of babysitting."

"Then you'll have to become a Bonnie B hermit," Jace said. "And never leave the ranch to avoid running into Bethany. So that means no rodeo next week, since she'll definitely be there to see her new sister-in-law perform. Oh, and you'll have to bury your phone so that you can't text Bethany under some pretext."

"But just till the baby comes," Billy said on a chuckle. "Since a baby is the last thing you want."

Again Theo caught his brothers sharing a glance. And he knew what that look meant too. That they didn't think Theo stood a chance. That he was too interested in Bethany McCreery to walk away.

Theo scowled. Why had he thought his brothers would be of help? He was actually more confused now.

Bandit let out a *woof*, his tail wagging excitedly. Was the pooch offering an opinion on the situation?

Billy glanced at his watch. "Good boy, Bandit," he said, bending down to give the dog a pat. "Who needs a watch when we have Bandit to tell us that the day camp bus should be pulling up to the stop right about now?"

Theo put back the muck rake he'd been holding—gripping like some kind of a lifeline—and the three of them left the barn, Bandit hurrying ahead to the ranch's long drive, tail wagging away in excitement. If only Theo had a dog's mysterious way of knowing what was coming.

"Time to put on my dad hat," Billy said, tipping up his Stetson. "Three teenagers are about to come barreling up the drive to raid the fridge for a snack before I have to drop them all off in three different places. *That* is the life of a dad."

"Unless you're me and it's still about changing diapers," Jace added with a grin.

"I wouldn't trade my life for anything," Billy added. "I might sound corny but being a dad is the best thing that has ever happened to me. Watching my kids grow up and become teenagers has given me a few gray hairs, but it is amazing watching these little babies become independent." He laughed. "And if the learner's permits don't give me gray hair, the dating definitely will. And with a fourth on the way, I couldn't be happier."

"Yup," Jace said with a nod. "Fatherhood changed me in the best in of ways. That a tiny little human who can't even talk yet can teach you so much about life and love— that's amazing. And hey, Frankie brought Tamara into my life, so I have to give him extra props."

Huh, Theo thought, taking all that in. He was about to ask his brothers if they missed being able to focus solely on the ranch, but he just heard the bus pulling to a stop and the door opening and closing. The sounds of chatter and laughter were heading in their direction. And then Billy's kids came up the path, talking a mile a minute, interrupting each other, laughing, teasing.

Theo adored his niece and nephews. Branson, the oldest at seventeen, still didn't have his license because he'd flunked his driver's test. According to Billy, Branson had been doing great on the road test, then noticed a girl he had a crush on going into the Gemstone Diner and took his eyes off the road long enough to almost swerve into an oncoming car. He'd try again in a few weeks.

Fifteen-year-old Nicky had recently gotten his learner's permit, and Billy and Charlotte had gone to bed each night since with their nerves stretched to the limit.

Then there was Jill, soon to turn fourteen and starting high school in the fall, begging to be allowed to wear makeup this summer so she could be a pro at it for the first day late next month. All three teens had the Abernathy green eyes, but they couldn't be more different from one another.

"You're dropping me at Kara's, right?" Branson asked his dad. Kara was the girl he'd failed his road test over.

"If a parent will be home—as we talked about," Billy countered.

Nicky and Jill snickered.

"Fine, yes, her mom will be home," Branson said.

It took Theo a minute to figure out why Billy cared if a parent would be home. Hormone-raging teenagers with huge crushes on each other home alone? Got it.

"Dad," Nicky said, "I have to be at Bronco Brick Oven Pizza at three forty-five for the lacrosse team's fundraiser.

Oh, and you're supposed to Venmo the payment to the assistant coach for the end-of-summer barbecue in August."

"Got it," Billy told his son.

"Dad, you can drop me off at Heather's before that, right?" Jill asked. "You know you always end up chatting away with other parents during drop-off. And can I adopt two kittens?" She gave her dad serious puppy-dog eyes. "A girl at camp has four left to find homes for. We'd be doing a good deed! Pleeeeeze, Daddy?"

"Listen, Jilly Bean. We have two cats already. And a dog. And three fish tanks. So that's gonna have to be a hard no."

"Can I get a bearded dragon for my birthday, then?" Jill asked. "Charlotte *loves* lizards."

Billy raised an eyebrow as his brothers swallowed their laughter. His fiancée was a marine biologist who loved sea creatures. Theo had never heard her mention lizards. "We'll talk about that."

"Yes!" Jill said. "That's not a no!"

"Dad, don't forget I need to get to camp an hour early tomorrow," Branson said. "The CITs are having a meeting."

"That means you two will need to get there an hour early too," Billy said to Nicky and Jill. "Unless Uncle Theo wants to take you before he goes to the first of many cattle auctions." Ah, the pleading look in his brother's eyes.

"Uncle Theo would love to," Theo told Nicky and Jill.

"Awesome!" Jill said, holding up her hand for a high five to Nicky, who was busy digging deep in his backpack for who knew what. Probably the source of the strange odor wafting out. Like a three-day-old half-eaten fast-food burger.

Jace leaned close to Theo. "At least you'll have a good

twelve years before you hit the teen stage. That's if you survive the terrible twos." He laughed. "Not that I'm looking forward to that. I've heard horror stories."

Theo swallowed. Terrible twos? If he did get involved with Bethany McCreery, the terrible twos were right around the corner.

He knew he was ready for a serious relationship. Marriage, even. But this? Babies and toddlers and teenagers depending on him? Needing him? For everything?

He loved his nephews and niece to pieces. But he just couldn't see himself in Jace's and Billy's roles. Not yet.

"I definitely shouldn't start something I can't finish," he whispered to Jace as the kids ran down the path to their house to grab drinks and snacks and very likely mess up the kitchen.

"Except when love gets you, you're gotten," Jace said, enjoying this a little too much.

Theo shook his head. "Who said anything about love? I had *one* date. And it wasn't even a date. It was a *walk*."

"A walk into Pastabilities for dinner," Billy reminded him. "That's a date." He gave his brothers a wave and started after his kids. "See ya later."

Theo wasn't *gotten*. But he had to admit that Bethany had been on his mind throughout this entire conversation. And not because they were talking about her. And her baby.

Because he couldn't stop thinking about her. Seeing her face and silky brown hair. Her big blue eyes. Her beautiful voice.

I'm not gotten, he told himself. *I'm just…*

Something.

Something he couldn't think about anymore or he'd drive himself crazy.

* * *

Almost a full day had passed since Bethany had told Theo that she was pregnant. Not a word from him.

As it would be tomorrow and the next day and…forever. *Right guy, wrong time*, she reminded herself.

Actually, he wasn't the right guy. The right guy would want a baby now. Particularly in five months. He'd be ready for fatherhood. Ready to share his life with his family.

You have to forget him, she told herself.

She'd had a group video chat with her two besties, Suzanna and Dana, last night when she had got home. They were both away, Suzanna visiting her sister who'd just had a baby, and Dana on vacation with her husband to celebrate their fifth wedding anniversary. Bethany had finally told them her big news, and the surprise and happiness on her friends' faces buoyed her. They made sure she knew that no matter what, they'd always be there for her and would throw her one heck of a baby shower.

She'd told them all about Theo too. Both had counseled her *not* to forget him, to give it a little time, to give *him* a little time. People, relationships evolved, they'd both said. She'd gone back and forth during a restless night in bed. *Forget him. Forget him not.*

All she knew was that sitting in the waiting room of her ob-gyn's office, her brother beside her, had her wistful. On one hand, she was grateful she wasn't here alone for her monthly checkup. She'd called Jake this morning to ask if he had some time to meet today, that she had something big to tell him. He'd appeared at her apartment door ten minutes later with bagels and veggie cream cheese. Elizabeth and her sisters had taken all five kids to the Bronco

Convention Center to watch them set up for the rodeo that would open this week. The Hawkins Sisters were performing, but they weren't practicing until later in the afternoon, so Jake had a couple of hours to himself.

His mouth had dropped open at the big news that he was going to be an uncle. She could see how truly happy he was for her, despite the less-than-ideal details.

"Are you going to tell Rexx?" he'd asked.

"I want to. But given the way he hung up on me when I called… The last thing he and his fiancée are going to want to hear is that his former bandmate is pregnant with his baby."

"No doubt," Jake had said. "But you should call him again. He is the father and he should know, period."

She'd nodded, in full agreement. It was one thing when no one knew. But now that she'd told her family, her bandmates were next. Rexx had cut Harry, Cord, and Petey from his life too—apparently the fiancée didn't think he should have any connection with his old life. Bethany and the Belters were meeting up in a few days to practice a few new songs that an upcoming bride and groom had put on their list; she'd tell them then. And call Rexx that night.

Right now, she just wanted to get through this appointment, to hear that all was well with her baby.

Earlier today, when she'd mentioned that she was going to her ob-gyn checkup alone, Jake had insisted on accompanying her. He'd shown up at her apartment to pick her up for the appointment bearing gifts: a book called *Your Pregnancy Month by Month*—which she already had—and a pink highlighter, soft orange pj's with little horses down the zipper, matching orange socks, and a furry stuffed sheep. He'd also gotten himself a T-shirt that read, Montana's Newest Uncle.

Bethany had burst into tears at how thoughtful her brother was, how supported she felt.

"Thanks for coming with me, Jake," she said. Here he was, a newlywed, father of five now, and he'd made time for his sister.

He squeezed her hand. "Of course. Anything, anytime. You just call me or text me, okay?"

"I really appreciate that," she said, tears misting her eyes. She tried to blink the tears away.

There were three other expectant moms in the room, all at least six months pregnant. And all with husbands. She knew because they were wearing wedding rings. And sitting with their arms or hands entwined.

She was with her brother.

At least she was here with someone who cared about her. Thank God for her family.

The nurse called her in for her checkup, and Bethany stood, grateful Jake would be waiting here for her. These appointments were nerve-racking. She just wanted to hear that her baby was okay.

Fifteen minutes later, in her paper scrubs, Dr. Rangely assured her all was well. Bethany breathed a huge sigh of relief and touched her hands to her belly, which felt bigger.

Pow!

Bethany gasped. "The baby just kicked again! He or she did that a few days ago for the first time. And now again!"

The doctor laughed. "It's the best feeling—except when you're nine months along and trying to sleep in any position you can and get a foot in the side."

Bethany smiled. "I can't wait for it all. The kicks, being nine months pregnant. Meeting my child."

"Five months will be here in a snap," Dr. Rangely said. She went over some basic details of what Bethany could expect in the next couple months. "Bronco Valley Hospital offers a wonderful one-day seminar for expectant parents. There's a one scheduled in August. The receptionist can give you an information packet on your way out."

"Great," Bethany said. "I definitely want to take that class."

She'd take it alone…but that was okay. She was going to be a single mother and needed to get used to doing baby-oriented activities on her own.

You can do this, she reminded herself. *You have the love and support of your family.*

And you'll be a mom—your dream come true.

But as she headed out to let her brother know all was well with the baby, she thought of Theo Abernathy.

That *you can't do*, she told herself. *Let it go. Let your fantasies of him go.*

She had to admit that, since their walk and dinner and the big reveal, she had fantasized that he'd come rushing to her apartment with a pronouncement that there was something special between them and he just couldn't walk away.

But he had.

Still, Bethany had always been optimistic. Which might be her downfall when it came to Theo Abernathy.

Chapter Six

The next morning, when Bethany was getting dressed for the Bronco Rodeo, she did a double take at her belly in the full-length mirror in the corner of her bedroom. She was definitely showing. The baby bump that was easily hidden by her flowy dresses and summer-weight cardigans now would be obvious no matter what.

She'd stood there for five minutes, marveling at the sight of her curved belly, turning left and right, trying on a bunch of different shirts and dresses to see how she looked.

Pregnant.

She settled on her favorite sundress and a meshy cardigan, since it could get cold in the Bronco Convention Center, where the rodeo would be held. Flat, comfy sandals, her lucky silver bangles on her wrist, and she was ready.

Last year her brother had picked her up, but this year he was carting five kids, and so she'd meet the McCreery-Hawkins crew and her parents at the rodeo. She was looking forward to spending the afternoon with her family. Tomorrow was the Fourth of July, a big deal in Bronco, with a barbecue that brought tons of people out, and the day after that was a fun event—the Favorite Pet Contest, which was cosponsored by Happy Hearts Animal Sanctuary, owned by her friend Daphne Taylor Cruise, and several other local businesses, including the company Daphne's husband, Evan, owned Bronco Ghost Tours, and his great-grandmother's very popular psychic shop, Wisdom by Winona.

Hmm. Bethany could use some psychic wisdom. Maybe she'd pay Winona Cobbs a visit if she had a booth set up at the rodeo. Her readings were free, and she often had pop-ups around town. The woman was in her nineties and engaged to be married to a wonderful man, an eightysomething charmer with a big smile, and surely she had some advice for Bethany. Or, at least, a prediction.

Bethany's burning question: Would she ever stop thinking about Theo Abernathy?

Two days now and no contact. He clearly didn't want to be friends. He didn't want to be *anything* with her, a pregnant woman.

She pushed away thoughts of him and drove to the convention center, wondering if she'd have to move her seat back from the steering wheel soon to accommodate her belly. The parking lot was crowded, but Bethany found a spot not too far from the entrance. She was grateful, because she was already tired and it wasn't even noon.

She found the big group of McCreerys and Hawkinses and settled into her seat. Suddenly she was hit with a powerful craving. "Who wants fried dough?" she asked. They were seated in the third row with a great view of the arena and the jumbotron, a huge video monitor to show closeups and announcements. The rodeo would start in fifteen minutes—just enough time to get her treat.

"Meeeee!" came the chorus of all five McCreery-Hawkins kids.

Bethany's mom laughed. "Dad and I will split one.

Sprinkle extra sugar on Dad's half," she added with a smile.

"Fried dough gives me a serious stomachache," Jake said, "so none for me. The kids can split two among them or they'll all have bellyaches."

"Got it," Bethany said, glad her brother wouldn't be sharing hers. She could eat an entire paper plate–sized fried dough herself. With a generous sprinkling of powdered sugar. "Be back in a jiff."

She got up, wondering if the folks seated nearby had noticed her belly. Probably not. She felt so conspicuous, though. As she wove her way down to the food area, she did notice a few people she knew from around town giving her a belly a glance. Soon, gossipers would take the news all over town. Bethany McCreery was pregnant. And single. There would be phone calls and texts, acquaintances not wanting to ask outright who the father was but hoping she'd share the info.

The story, from the sperm bank to Rexx and the surprise pregnancy, was one she couldn't imagine telling people. She'd gotten it out to those closest to her, and that was enough.

The smell of burgers and fries and pizza and popcorn and fried dough took her attention as she entered the crowded area with the food booths. There was a longish line for the fried dough stand, since it was the only one.

And who was coming from the opposite direction to get in that line at the exact moment she was?

Theo Abernathy.

For a moment she was mesmerized by the sight of him. The ole long, tall drink of water. Muscles galore. An untucked Western shirt with pearl buttons, dark-wash jeans that hugged his hips in a way that had her swallowing. His thick brown hair sexily tousled as he took off his Stetson in a kind of Western greeting.

He looked flustered.

She *felt* flustered.

"Craving?" he asked, then looked even more flustered, as if he wasn't sure he should even bring up the subject of her pregnancy. His gaze dropped to her belly for a moment, and he tilted his head.

"I'm showing more today," she said.

"How are you feeling?" he asked. "I've been wondering. According to my brother Billy, his ex-wife had bad morning sickness with each pregnancy and she was tired a lot."

Hmm. That must mean he'd told his brother. *Brothers*, probably. And maybe his sisters too. Which meant he was talking about her. That was interesting—and made her happier than it should have. Was he getting their advice? She wondered what they'd said.

Stay far away!

Theo, you're thirty-five. It's time for a family, anyway.

She also wondered why he was asking. The man had practically turned green when she told him she was pregnant. She'd think he'd avoid the topic altogether.

Theo Abernathy was a nice guy, plain and simple. But asking how she was feeling told her loud and clear that he cared. That he was interested in the biggest thing in her life right now.

And that pulled her right back in.

"I got lucky with morning sickness," she said. "I'm rarely bothered by it at all. But I do get tired, particularly in the late afternoons. The last two weddings I performed at, I needed a stool on stage just in case and ended up using it quite a bit. Luckily, I sing a lot of ballads, and sitting and slow songs go together."

He seemed to be taking that in, as if picturing her on stage, sitting on a stool and belting out "Endless Love" and "Because You Loved Me."

"Well, you look beautiful," he said, then his eyes widened and she knew he hadn't meant to say that. "Glowing," he added fast.

She couldn't help but smile. The fact that she was expecting didn't seem to have cooled his attraction to her. *That* was interesting. And made her heart flutter. "A perk of pregnancy. My skin has never looked better. And thank you."

He nodded and was quiet for a moment. "I love fried dough," he said, upping his chin at the huge sign above the booth. "With a lot of powdered sugar."

It seemed so clear to her that he wanted to say more. And not about fried dough. But like him, she felt like she had to keep things to small talk.

"Me too. I'm getting a bunch for my family to split and an entire one for myself."

They inched up in line, standing beside each other. Like they were together.

It was their turn, so he gestured for her to go ahead. She placed her order, and once she had her fried dough on a cardboard tray, there was no reason to stick around. But walking away from Theo wasn't so easy. She could stand here and talk about her cravings all day.

Him included.

Sigh.

"Well, nice to see you," she said—awkwardly.

Guess you don't want to be friends, she added silently and felt herself frowning.

"I'll carry the tray to your seat," he rushed to say.

Oh, Theo, she thought. *We clearly feel the same way about each other, but not about the giant thing keeping us apart.*

Why prolong the agony?

"That's okay. It's light," she added, lifting the tray up for good measure.

"If you start craving cheese fries, I know where the best booth is for that," he said. "Crinkle-cut and extra crispy. Just shoot me a text and your seat number and I'll bring some over."

The man liked her—really liked her. That she was pregnant and he liked his life exactly as it was had to messing with him. In five months, he couldn't have her *and* life as he knew it. So avoiding her was the right thing.

"Sounds like something a friend would do," she said before she could shut her big trap. Why had she come out with that? That was goading him. And she didn't want to do that.

"Sorry," she said. "It slipped out. You have every right to keep your distance. It's the smart thing to do, actually."

The air-conditioning vent had blown a swath of her long hair in her face, and since she held the tray in both hands, he reached out to move the strand back, his gaze on hers.

"Smart, maybe," he said. "And just as hard as I knew it would be. It's been rough not calling to see how you are, how you're feeling. To just…talk."

She really, really, really liked how straightforward he was. That he just said it.

She wondered if he'd add something. That they should *at least* be friends. But he didn't.

A bit dejected, even though it was for the best, she offered a tight smile. "I'd better get back to the hungry crowd with their treats before the Hawkins Sisters are introduced."

She turned and hurried through the crowd, her heart finally slowing a bit when she was a good distance from the booth. From the man who'd kept her awake the past few nights.

She closed her eyes for a second to try to blink Theo Abernathy away and then lifted her chin and walked to her seat. Her nieces and nephews clapped at the sight of her, their sweet excitement giving her heart a lift. She sat down just as the announcer introduced rodeo superstar Ross Burris. He rode out on his horse, waving his Stetson at the crowd, which was cheering and wolf whistling, none louder than his champ brother Jack and Jack's wife, Stephanie. She couldn't help but notice that Ross's eyes were on one particular person in the first row—his new bride, Celeste, a sports broadcaster who was solely a spectator today so that she could concentrate on her husband and his family in the ring.

The love in his gaze was so touching that Bethany felt a little ache of longing in her chest.

She ripped off a piece of her fried dough, the powdered sugar sticking to her fingers, and took a bite. All she could think was that Theo was probably doing the exact same thing in his own seat. She glanced around, sure she wouldn't spot him in the crowded bleachers, but there he was, sitting a section over and up two rows with his family.

So close—and yet very far.

* * *

For the past couple of hours, Theo had been half watching the rodeo riders and half trying to come up with excuses for going over to where Bethany was sitting. She was on the end of her row, which would make it easy to stand on the stairs and talk for a bit. He'd considered bringing her the cheese fries even though she hadn't texted. Given how awkward things had been on the fried dough line and her quick getaway, he hadn't been expecting to hear from her.

He could go say hi to a few of the Bonnie B ranch hands, who were sitting with a group in the row in front of hers. Then he'd just "happen to see her" and stop to say hello.

And then what? He had to stop this. It was bad enough that he was so drawn to a woman who was completely wrong for him. If they weren't friends and they weren't dating, he had no reason to stop and say hello.

He slid down in his seat, feeling sulky, and tried to focus on the arena, which had cleared for the next performance. A few workers were setting up, though Theo couldn't imagine what the little stage and podium were about. Or the red runner being rolled out to the stage. A worker carried a huge floor vase of white roses and set it beside the podium.

Suddenly, the wedding march blasted from the speakers. That sure got everyone's attention. What the heck was going on?

"Someone's getting married?" his mother asked, surprise lighting her face. "I love weddings!"

"Maybe it's an engagement announcement!" his sister Stacy said. "Remember how Dylan very publicly declared his love for Robin on the jumbotron back in February? How romantic was that?"

Theo had to agree that Dylan Sanchez had won the grand-gesture-of-the-year award. The new rancher hadn't been part of the rodeo; he'd been doing a live promotion for his car dealership when things took a very unexpected turn. The jumbotron had flashed, "Bronco Motors Car Deals for Cowboys" as Dylan had trotted around the arena on horseback, announcing the specials his dealership was offering that week. But then Dylan had suddenly veered from the live commercial. As the camera zoomed in on his face, he'd told the audience that he had an opportunity for one lucky recipient.

The cameras had then zoomed in on Robin, sitting in the stands, a close-up of her stunned face appearing on the jumbotron. Dylan raced into the stands and proposed, thousands at the rodeo cheering and clapping and wolf whistling.

All the Abernathys had been moved by that moment, no one more than Robin.

"Someone must have stolen Dylan's excellent grand-gesture idea," Jace said. He slid an arm around his beloved, Tamara, holding baby Frankie, giving his son a kiss on his cheek.

"What could possibly top what Dylan did?" Billy asked. "He'll go down in history."

Theo wished *he* could make some kind of grand gesture to Bethany. But again, to accomplish what? A grand apology for not being ready for a family of his own? For not staying far, far away when he should have? For pursuing her, anyway? Of course, at her brother's wedding, he hadn't known she was actually pregnant. In the back of his mind, he must have been thinking that if things worked out between them, he could convince her to wait a few years. He liked how that took him off the hook—a little, anyway.

The camera was now aimed right at an internal gate. Something was definitely about to happen. Had the wedding march music gotten louder? Sure seemed that way.

From where Theo was sitting, he could see the gate open, and it seemed like everyone was holding their breath, riveted, waiting for what was coming.

Suddenly, a man in a tux and black Stetson and a woman in a wedding gown entered the arena, both on horses. Theo's mom gasped. So did he and his entire family.

They all stood up to make sure they were seeing what they were plainly seeing.

When the jumbotron showed them close up, the Abernathys' mouths all dropped open.

Dylan Sanchez and Theo's sister Robin were on those horses.

"Okay, Dylan and Robin just outdid *themselves*," Stacy said, her eyes misty.

"Did you know about this?" Theo asked his parents.

Both Bonnie and Asa shook their heads. "News to us!" his mother said.

"How did they manage to keep this a surprise?" Billy asked.

"Right?" Jace said. "A pop-up wedding at the rodeo!"

"So romantic!" Tamara and Charlotte said in unison.

"And we're getting a new son-in-law!" Bonnie said to her husband, hand over her heart.

"Not to mention a family discount at Dylan's car dealership," Asa exclaimed on a chuckle.

The jumbotron flashed with "Something Old? Check. Something New? Check. Something Borrowed? Uh-oh! Something Blue? Check."

A whole bunch of people were rushing to the fence to offer the bride something borrowed—from hats to rodeo pennants and giant foam fingers. But Bronco's mayor's wife, Penny Smith, was already in the arena, handing over her pearl necklace, which Theo had heard her husband, Rafferty, had given her for their thirtieth anniversary. Theo had also heard people in town saying that the necklace was magical—that it brought those who came into contact with it forever love. Penny had temporarily lost the necklace, and as it had made its way around town, at least two couples—Shep Dalton and Rylee Parker, and Ross Burris and Celeste Montgomery—had fallen under its spell. Theo wasn't one to believe in legends and magic, but what did he know?

A close-up of the pearl necklace being clasped around Robin's neck by her groom-to-be appeared on the jumbotron.

The crowd went wild, cheering and clapping.

Theo glanced over at Bethany. She and her entire family were on their feet, all of them chatting excitedly and the kids pointing. She turned to look at him, and they locked eyes. She seemed to be mouthing something—he was pretty sure it was *Congratulations*.

He mouthed back a thank-you with a question in his expression and a shrug to indicate that this was a total surprise.

"Folks," the announcer said over the loudspeakers. "Surprise! You're all invited to a pop-up wedding right here at the Bronco Rodeo. This happy couple will say their I dos right now!"

The arena gate opened, and out came a minister on a white horse wearing a bow tie. That got the crowd going wild again.

And then, in front of thousands, Robin Abernathy and Dylan Sanchez vowed to love, honor, and cherish each other forever. Theo felt his eyes get a little misty. He glanced at his mom, who had tears streaming down her cheeks. His sister Stacy was full-out bawling.

When the minister pronounced Dylan and Robin husband and wife, the two gave each other a sweet, soulful kiss, and then the crowd roared again.

"Bethany McCreery, come on down!" the announcer called. "The bride and groom have requested that you sing their favorite song!"

Theo looked over at Bethany, who seemed surprised and touched. Given how mesmerized he'd been by her angelic voice at her brother's wedding, *he* was hardly surprised that the happy couple would want her to perform the first song.

He felt something shift in his chest, in the region of his heart, as she hurried down the stairs and was ushered through a gate into the arena. Just what was going on inside him? What did he feel for this woman who was supposed to be off-limits?

A lot, he was beginning to realize. He couldn't take his eyes off Bethany as she was led to a mike set up in the center, the newlyweds facing each other, holding hands, their wedding bands glinting in the summer sunshine.

The minister whispered into Bethany's ear. She nodded

and smiled, and then music began playing, a song Theo recognized. An oldie but goodie.

As Bethany began singing about letting someone into your heart and taking a chance, again the yearning and passion in her voice had the entire audience rapt. No one more so than Theo.

All the love in the air—and his own sister as the surprise bride—must be getting to him.

Because he couldn't imagine walking away from this woman. And he wasn't going to.

Chapter Seven

While Bethany was singing to the newlyweds and about three thousand guests at the pop-up wedding, she noticed Theo coming down the bleacher steps toward the arena floor as though he couldn't stay away from her another second. But then she realized that *all* the Abernathys, including his aunt and uncle and cousins and their spouses, were right there with him—to congratulate the happy couple.

They'd all stopped just inside the gate, since the bride and groom were slow dancing on the red aisle runner. Bethany noticed that Robin and Dylan hadn't taken their eyes off each other.

When she finished the song, she was stunned by the standing ovation, then realized it was more for the newlyweds. She shook her head at herself with a smile and gave a bow toward the couple, then to the crowd. As the Abernathys hurried to hug Robin and Dylan, she headed for the gate.

"Beautiful song," said a male voice from behind her.

She turned, hand on the gate, to find Theo standing just a few feet away.

"I'm amazed that you can just sing like that with no notice and in front of so many people," he added.

"I'm a little shy generally, but not when it comes to singing. I get lost in the music, in the lyrics, and I'm transported."

"I can tell," he said.

"Thanks, Theo. That's really nice of you to say." She bit her lip, so...schoolgirl around this man. "So was this a surprise for your family too?" she asked to get them on a neutral topic.

"Total surprise. We had no idea. But given Dylan's previous gesture at the rodeo, we should have figured." He smiled and shook his head. "Somehow, it managed to be really romantic."

Bethany laughed. "Right? I got all teary when they recited their vows."

"Okay, I might have too. My mother and sister were sobbing."

Bethany glanced over at the crowd hovering around the newlyweds. The Sanchez family was there too, and they were all talking and hugging and laughing.

A pang hit her in the chest. She'd likely never be that bride, basking in the love of two families joined together in happy celebration.

She felt a frown tugging her lips and sucked in a breath. Bethany always had to brace herself when she prepared to go on stage at weddings. The always-the-wedding-singer-never-the-bride feeling had been hitting her hard this past year—particularly the past four months. But at this surprise wedding, she'd been unable to prepare herself. The silver lining was her awareness of the passion in her voice as she'd sung the bride's favorite song.

She had to change the subject fast. "I actually have my

own connection to the Sanchez family. I live in one of the apartments above the hair salon Denise Sanchez owns."

He smiled and nodded. "It's like *one* degree of separation in Bronco. Everyone knows everyone."

Okay, maybe that wasn't such a change of subject. Now she and Theo were connected by a Bronco Valley hair salon. Every time she pulled into her spot in the small lot of the building, she'd think of the Sanchez matriarch and her romantic son, Dylan, and his bride, Robin, Theo's sister. And that would make her think of him. She sighed.

She took off her cardigan and tied it around her waist. "Warm out. But a nice breeze." Now that was a change of subject. Nice and dull. Impersonal.

He studied her with concern. "Can I get you a cold drink? Iced tea? Water? Juice?"

That got a smile out of her—and made her feel equally wistful. "You know, for someone who doesn't want to be friends, you're doting on me a bit."

Sometimes she wished she had more of a filter. Was it the pregnancy that was making her more forthright? Saying what was on her mind? Probably.

He seemed flustered again, which tempered her confusion over what he did or didn't want where the two of them were concerned. "We're already friends, so I might as well dote."

Good comeback, she thought. They *did* feel like friends. *Oh, heck.*

"Well, I'm happy to be your friend," she said. "Because you sure seem nice, Theo Abernathy."

"My last few girlfriends wouldn't agree." His cheeks reddened a bit as though he hadn't meant to say that out loud. They were certainly a pair.

She could feel her eyes widen at that tidbit. "Because they'd figured at thirty-five, you'd be ready for marriage and family?"

He nodded. "They just couldn't understand. 'You're not twenty-five,' my last girlfriend would snap at me. 'Haven't you gotten doing whatever you want, whenever you want out of your system?'"

Well, honestly, Theo, haven't you?

"I feel how I feel, right?" he asked. "At least I know I'm ready for marriage. That's a biggie too. I'm definitely ready to share my life with my soulmate. But not giving the ranch everything I've got because I have little ones who need all of me? That I'm not ready for."

Surely he understood that his brothers managed to do just that. Life was about balance. "Well, I do know what you mean about giving your work your all. It's a rare day like today when I have hours to myself to enjoy a rodeo. Usually if I'm not hustling for new wedding gigs, I'm performing."

"And even today you ended up working—for free, now that I think about it." He tilted his head. "As a representative of the bride's family, I'd like to make that up to you."

She put up her hand. "You don't have to. Really, I—"

"At least let me buy you lunch," he said. "I know which booth has the best corn dog. I'd take you somewhere much fancier than a rodeo stand—like the Association—but my family just made impromptu plans to get together with the Sanchezes at the ranch house to toast the newlyweds." He shrugged and leaned in closer. "To tell you the truth, I'd actually take a corn dog over a fancy restaurant any day."

She smiled. "Honestly, if I'm being treated, I'd take the fancy restaurant."

His warm smile went straight into her heart.

"Rain check, then," he said.

For a moment, they just stood there, gazing at each other like lovebirds without saying anything.

She had to put a stop to that pronto.

Bethany extended her hand. "To friendship," she said.

He slipped his warm, strong hand around hers. "To friendship."

Everything tingled. All her nerve endings.

She had to get away from this man and yet couldn't move. Couldn't drag her eyes off him.

"I'll be at the Favorite Pet Contest the day after tomorrow," she said fast. "I love seeing all the dogs. You going?" The contest was her favorite annual event of the town's July Fourth week festivities. It was being held in a large air-conditioned room in the Bronco Convention Center, since it could get very hot in July in Montana and the pets needed to be kept comfortable. There was an outdoor area where folks could walk their dog entrants too. A huge board of all the hopefuls with their photos and names was at the exit, and people would vote for their very favorite pet by marking an X under their photo. At the end of the day, Mayor Rafferty Smith would announce the winner, who'd receive a generous gift certificate to Bronco Pets Emporium.

"And miss the goofy rodents and occasional bearded dragon? I'll definitely be there."

"I'll see you there, then," she said.

He seemed about to say something but then clamped his mouth shut. She had the feeling he was going to offer to pick her up, that they could go together, but that probably seemed too date-like.

How exactly was this friendship thing supposed to work when he gave her butterflies and just the touch of his hand on hers made her toes tingle?

"Theo, we're heading out," a voice called.

They both turned. His brother Jace, holding the cutest baby, held up a hand in greeting.

She smiled back. "Well, I'll let you go."

And she really had to.

But having shaken on friendship, how exactly was she going to get this man out of her heart?

The two families had decided to celebrate the newly-weds with a quick toast in the parklike backyard of the Bonnie B. The bride and groom were there, stealing a kiss behind a stately maple tree, and all Theo's siblings and their significant others and children, plus the Sanchezes— Dylan's parents, four siblings, their spouses, fiancées and his adorable niece. Plus Dylan's great-uncle Stanley and his bride-to-be, Winona Cobbs, the town's resident psychic.

When he'd been talking to Bethany in the arena, Theo had been thinking about inviting her along to the party, but that seemed a little beyond the scope of their new friendship. Not to mention that Theo could only imagine the grilling he'd get from his brothers—and his sisters— if she was his plus-one.

He glanced around, summer itself decorating the yard for the impromptu occasion with the brilliant green grass and beautiful gardens his mother loved tending to. Bronco, Montana, had gifted them with gorgeous weather for the rodeo and the party—sunny and breezy and a tempera-ture in the low seventies now. Bandit was enjoying a patch of sunshine in his dog bed on the deck, two kids petting him and chatting him up, which he seemed to be enjoying, since he rolled onto his belly for a rub. The kids were delighted.

He looked around for his parents and found Asa and Bonnie chatting with Denise and Aaron Sanchez on the deck, each holding a glass of champagne. His mother was still misty-eyed, the softy. Theo heard the word *reception* a few times; he had no doubt they were planning a grand celebration. Stacy and his brothers were in a big circle on the grass with Dylan's siblings: Camilla and her husband, Jordan Taylor; Felix and his fiancée, Shari Lormand; Sofia and her husband, Boone Dalton, a fellow rancher; and Dante and his fiancée, Eloise Taylor, sister of Billy's fiancée and cousin-in-law of Camilla Sanchez-Taylor. Lots of kids were running around the backyard.

Theo watched parents being constantly interrupted by their children, whether toddlers or big kids or teens. His nephew Branson apparently wanted to slip out to meet his friends and had gotten a no from his dad—*three* times in the past hour. Niece Jill asked why she couldn't have a teensy sip of champagne when everyone else had a glass, and other nephew Nicky had to be told twice to take off his headphones and engage with the guests.

Meanwhile, Jace's son, Frankie, had grabbed on to Camilla Sanchez-Taylor's hair as she'd been passing by— and still wouldn't let go. That was getting to be Frankie's trademark move. A small crowd had gathered, trying everything from tickling Frankie's tummy and neck to get him to release her hair to attempting to peel his fingers off without a hank being ripped out. At this moment, Camilla was still held prisoner by a twenty-two-pound cherub.

One of the kids had climbed that stately maple and now couldn't get down, requiring her dad to climb up after her.

No, thanks, Theo thought. He was one of the only ones at this pop-up get-together who was enjoying his champagne and chatting with the Sanchezes without constant interruption.

"She's free!" Jace called out.

Theo glanced over to see poor Camilla dart over to safety behind her husband her hair askew. She was smiling but rubbing her head.

"Theo, Theo, Theo," said a crackly voice from behind him.

Theo turned to find Winona Cobbs eyeing him. Winona was a marvel. She had her long white hair in a braid and wore a purple Stetson and a purple pantsuit with fringe along the hem of her jacket. And silver cowboy boots.

"Afternoon, Winona," he said, taking off his hat. "So I figure you knew about the wedding."

"In spirit, sure," she said cryptically. Which was her way. He was still trying to figure out what she meant when she added, "You only think you know what you want."

He studied Winona, waiting for her to elaborate. Instead she simply walked away and joined Stanley by the patio table, where Theo's mother had set out a platter of treats that she and his father had paid a small fortune to a few town cafés and bakeries to deliver pronto—at least three dozen treats from Kendra's Cupcakes and an huge assortment of cookies and scones from Bronco Java and Juice. The kids had beelined for the table and were now sitting on the steps of the deck, frosting on several little noses.

Theo had to admit, when they were quiet and adorable

like that, he could almost see having a child of his own. Someday down the line.

He felt eyes on him and turned to find Winona Cobbs staring at him—hard. No expression whatsoever.

You only think you know what you want.

What did that mean? Theo might not be the biggest believer in psychics—if at all—but he'd heard enough about Winona's spot-on comments and predictions that had come true to know that when she did say something, folks took her very seriously.

And Winona had been around a long, long time. Ninety-plus years. She'd lived a hard life and had gone through more before she was eighteen than a lot of people ever did. Like himself. He knew he had it easy.

He thought about Bethany, wondering if she was chasing after a gig as she'd mentioned earlier about either working or looking for work. Darn it. He'd been trying not to think about her, and now she was on his mind again.

They were now friends. Officially. He'd never wanted to kiss any of his female friends, though.

He'd also never wanted to attend the Bronco Favorite Pet Contest so badly. Bethany would be there. And therefore, so would he. Not that he'd lied when he said he liked seeing the residents' pets. He did. But spending time with Bethany while looking at gerbils and guinea pigs and a lot of dogs was the big draw.

He felt an arm sneak around his. He turned to find his sister Stacy beside him.

"Looks like we're the last two standing," Stacy said, pushing her brown hair behind her shoulders. "Who's gonna fall first, you or me?"

He laughed. "I'm on the market, so it's anyone's guess."

"Really?" she asked, her eyes lighting up. "Actively looking for your Ms. Right?"

"I've been for a while now," he said, sipping his champagne. "I *am* thirty-five," he added.

"Wow, Theo Abernathy, settled down with a wife and two-point-five kids. I can't see it, but I want to." She grinned.

"Well, at this point I'm more interested in the wife than in the children."

Bethany's beautiful face flashed into his mind. And her baby bump.

He quickly took another sip of champagne.

"Not ready?" Stacy repeated. "Why? You did say you were thirty-five. Marriage and kids are the next step, right?"

"But what about the ranch? And let's say I wanted to jet off to Rome for pasta?" he asked. "For chicken Milanese?" Where that had come from, he had no idea. But suddenly— no, lately—he felt like he needed to justify his feelings.

She raised an eyebrow. "Um, what? When have you ever flown to Italy for linguine?"

"But I *could*," he said. "Because I don't have responsibilities for children. I can take off at a moment's notice. I'm not ready to give that up."

She chuckled. "I see. You do realize women your age will likely want kids. I mean, if you date, say, a thirty-year-old single woman…"

He let out a sigh. "Yes, that's been made clear."

The issue there was that he enjoyed dating women his age or close to it. Same life experiences. Same wavelength. Same references.

Stacy looked pointedly at him. "You wouldn't let the right woman get away because she wants kids now and you don't, though. Right?"

"But wouldn't that make her the *wrong* woman?" he asked.

Stacy lifted her champagne glass. "Touché," she said. "Hey, if you're not ready, you're not ready. But maybe you just *think* you're not."

Winona's words came back to him, making him frown. *You think you know what you want...*

Eh. He knew what he wanted. And didn't want.

He definitely wanted Bethany.

And he *definitely* didn't want kids. Not yet.

The problem was that Bethany McCreery was a package deal: her and a baby.

Which was why they'd shaken on friendship.

But he also didn't want to be just friends with Bethany. He wanted more.

A big conundrum. He looked around for the purple cowboy hat and easily spotted Winona Cobbs dancing with her fiancé to Frank Sinatra via Bluetooth speaker. Maybe he should pay Winona's psychic shop a visit. Get her words of wisdom. Ask her outright what a man in his situation was supposed to do.

Yes, maybe he'd go see Winona Cobbs for a reading.

Jeez, was he really considering going to a psychic for her thoughts on his life? What was happening to him?

Just how bad did he have it for Bethany McCreery?

Chapter Eight

Bethany loved the Fourth of July—the patriotism and fireworks and barbecue, which she'd attended yesterday with her family—but she'd been eager for today to arrive. She'd be meeting up with Theo at the Favorite Pet Contest in the convention center. As she walked among the tables with many cages containing everything from rabbits to hamsters to snakes and lizards, she tried not to look around for him.

But her gaze kept scanning the crowd. Theo didn't seem to be here yet. Her new nieces were exclaiming over two long-haired guinea pigs, clearly taken by their funny antics. Bethany was charmed by all the dogs being walked around, many still wearing red, white, and blue bandannas. She didn't have any pets since she traveled a lot and was gone for long stretches during the day or evening, but one day, when her baby was a few years old, maybe she'd finally adopt a dog of her own.

Bethany was eyeing a snake slithering up a branch in its tall cage when she noticed elderly lovebirds Winona and Stanley beside her, smiling at the long-haired guinea pig. Its name, according to the information sheet on the side of the cage, was Lovey.

"Morning, Winona, Stanley," Bethany said with a smile. "Enjoying the pets?"

Stanley grinned. "Yes, very much. I love all creatures—even mosquitoes."

Winona chuckled. "I wouldn't be surprised if one of the contest entrants was a bunch of mosquitoes with names. Spike, Buzzy, George."

"A mosquito named George," Stanley said, then gave his fiancée a kiss on the cheek. "Love it."

They laughed, and right there, in the middle of the room, Stanley took Winona's hand and twirled her around.

Bethany watched them in awe. Stanley, so tall and handsome in his vest and bolo tie, and Winona in her trademark purple, including her cowboy hat. They were clearly so in love—and there wasn't a bit of the tension that she'd noticed over the past couple of months. Bethany was friendly with Winona's great-granddaughter Vanessa Cruise John, and had heard little updates about the couple. Apparently over the winter, Winona had had cold feet about actually getting married. Stanley had wanted to set a date, but Winona insisted they wait until the time was right, saying, "Love cannot be rushed." But in March, they had set a date. Stanley was so excited and started planning a big wedding, even though Winona would have been fine with a justice of the peace at the Bronco Town Hall. But then for a while, there had seemed to be tension between them—something to do with Winona's harrowing past and whether Winona wanted to marry at all.

Bethany didn't know many of the details, but she'd heard that Winona had been an unwed teenaged mother who'd been told her baby had died—and had no idea until decades later that the child had really been placed for adoption. She and her daughter, Daisy, with whom she now lived, had only been reunited a few years ago—after a seventy-plus-year separation. There had to be a very heartrending story there.

It was one of the reasons why Bethany had been so happy to hear last month that Winona had assured her fiancé she did want to marry him. The wedding was set for just a couple of weeks from now, and Bethany and her band had been hired to perform. She couldn't wait to serenade the wonderful couple.

If Winona could find love in her nineties and be a first-time bride...

Bethany had been very touched to be invited to Winona's bridal shower last month. There had been so many women there that she hadn't gotten to talk to Winona much, but the happiness on the dear woman's face was unmistakable. Winona's daughter, Beatrix, had given Bethany a song list for the wedding, and she'd been practicing some of the ones she didn't know by heart. Bethany wanted to make sure she got every song just right. She and her band would get together a couple of times over the next two weeks to rehearse.

Winona slipped her arm through Bethany's and pulled her aside. "A baby is a blessing, no matter the circumstances."

Bethany gasped. How did—

Ah, of course. Winona *was* psychic. But now that Bethany had an obvious baby bump—however small at just four months—her flowy sundresses weren't hiding it.

As Bethany looked at this beautiful, strong woman, she thought of Winona being told her baby had died when she was just seventeen. Suddenly, she wished she knew more of the story—not because it was any of her business, but because Winona meant so much to Bethany and to the whole town, really. She did know that the Abernathy family was involved. Maybe she could ask Theo.

Winona winked at her and squeezed Bethany's hand, then returned to Stanley, who was waving at a long-eared black-and-white rabbit in a large crate. Stanley turned and kissed her so tenderly on the cheek, gazing at her with such affection.

Bethany sighed. Everyone around her seemed to be finding love and getting married. Not that she didn't feel blessed—she was so excited to meet her little one.

But love did seem to have passed her by...

Of course, at that moment, whom did she see but Theo Abernathy in his black Stetson, Western shirt and hip-hugging dark jeans. Her entire body vibrated for a moment, and it had nothing to do with her pregnancy. Then again, she had serious hormones coursing through her.

Her reaction to Theo was more about her being a red-blooded woman.

The moment he saw her his face lit up, and right there, Bethany knew she was sunk, that she really did have feelings for this man. And unless he was just really happy about having her as a friend, that lit-up face, the twinkling green eyes, the way he wove through the crowd to get to her, told her he had strong feelings for her too.

She got another hand squeeze, this time from Theo.

"The Bonnie B already has a dog, but all these pups make me want to adopt five more. Maybe ten."

Bethany smiled. "I know what you mean. I saw one of those little sausage dogs and immediately wanted to scoop him up."

Theo nodded. "Small dogs, big dogs, I love them all. Through my brother Billy's fiancée, Charlotte, I'll be related, albeit distantly, to the woman who's cosponsoring the pet contest—Daphne Taylor Cruise. She owns Happy Hearts Animal Sanctuary."

"I love that place! I actually go whenever I'm feeling down or need to count my blessings. All those sweet horses and cows and pigs and dogs and cats who needed rescuing and a good home. Last time I was there, there was a family of ducks and a rabbit that just came in. But I think the rabbit got adopted because I saw one here—someone's favorite pet—who looked just like that bunny."

He smiled. "Daphne is a marvel. She comes from a huge family of cattle ranchers but is a vegetarian herself and an animal rights activist. Took her a long time to make her father accept that. Oh—and when I arrived, I saw you talking to Winona Cobbs. Daphne's husband, Evan Cruise, is Winona's great-grandson. Her psychic shop, Wisdom by Winona, is actually on the property of his ghost tours business."

"I adore Winona," she said. At some point, she'd ask if he knew what had happened between Winona and her first love, who was an Abernathy. But right now, she wanted to explore the pet contest with Theo.

"To be honest, that woman scares me a little," he said. "She *knows* stuff. I never believed in psychics or 'gifts' of that nature, but Winona sure has proven herself time and again."

Bethany nodded. "I'm so tempted to go to her for a reading. But she might blurt out whether I'm having a boy or girl, and I want it to be a surprise."

"I do like surprises," Theo said. "But yeah, I'm tempted too. Just to get some feedback on myself that's not from my very opinionated siblings."

She laughed. "Do they know you well?"

"Both fortunately and unfortunately—yes." He chuckled, then bent to look in the cage of a pet rat named Gizmo.

"Are rats *pets*?" he asked. "News to me."

She smiled. "I think my brother had a pet rat once."

"Um, what *is* that?" he asked, pointing at something in a cage across the aisle.

Bethany peered in. "I think it's a cat. A hairless cat!" They both read the info sheet. It was indeed a hairless cat, named Lavinia.

They spent the next hour roaming around, admiring the dogs on leashes, the graceful cats and adorable kittens, the birds and rodents and all the rest.

"Craving anything?" he asked. "Tacos from the food truck? Corn dog?"

She smiled. "I actually would love a chicken taco with the works and a strawberry lemonade with ice."

"I'm on it. Why don't you sit and rest for a bit, and I'll be right back."

He escorted her to a bench in the outdoor area, and she was never so grateful to sit down. She set her sunhat beside her, but just then, a border collie on a long lead snatched her hat and ran off. It happened so fast she didn't think its owner, engaged in conversation, even noticed.

"I'd go chase that down for you," Theo said with a grin, "but I doubt you want a slobbered-on, chewed hat. But no worries. I'm on that too. Back in a jiff."

My hero, she thought before she could stop herself. He was back in ten minutes with a cardboard tray of four tacos, two lemonades, and a bag dangling off his arm.

"For you, m'lady," he said with a half bow.

For maybe the first time in her life, Bethany McCreery giggled.

He set down the tray beside her. "Okay, be on the look-out for any taco-stealing dogs. These are definitely more enticing than a straw hat," he said, gesturing toward the delicious-smelling tacos. Then he reached into the bag and pulled out a hat almost identical to the dognapped one and set it on her head. "Lovely."

Oh, Theo, she thought. *Why are you everything I want when I'm everything you* don't *want?*

"Thank you," she said. "Very much. You sure are a nice friend."

He smiled and sat beside the tray, then handed her a taco. He pointed out the choices of taco sauce, and for the next fifteen minutes they ate and sipped their lemonades and people- and dog-watched, sharing funny thoughts and imagining what the dogs' names were. She could sit here with him forever.

But all the happy families passing by had her feeling so wistful. Lots of couples with baby strollers or babies in chest carriers. Many toddlers between parents with a hand holding each. Couples in love with arms around each other. All manner of people holding hands.

And then there was Bethany. Alone but with…a friend.

You aren't alone, she reminded herself and immediately brightened. A hand went to her belly.

As they finished the last of the tacos and drained the lemonades, he pointed out every dog and owner who looked alike, making her laugh.

But if she sat here for another minute, she might burst into tears, thanks to her raging hormones and her crush on this man. It was time to get off this bench and move along—literally and figuratively. At least if they were going to look at more pets, they'd be focused on more than themselves.

As she thanked Theo again—for lunch and the hat—she was dying to lean over and kiss him, even on his cheek.

She wanted more. So much more. To be held by him. To kiss him on his lips.

She wanted him. And couldn't have him.

She stood but then dropped right back down. She felt... not quite faint, but not quite right either. All that walking and bending and kneeling down to pet dogs and look in cages, plus the hot sun by late afternoon, had done a number on Bethany, despite their twenty-minute rest on the bench.

She moved both hands to the back of her waist to give the tender spots a rub. She couldn't reach where it really felt achy.

"Are you all right?" Theo asked, his eyes on her with concern. "Do you need to move to a shadier bench?"

"That and a back rub," she said, then immediately felt herself blush. She hoped he wouldn't take that as fishing for a massage. But the thought of Theo's strong hands rubbing her back—ooh, la-la.

He peered at her and took her frown—directed at herself and her big mouth—for pain. "Let me take you home. I'll have your car dropped off for you."

She tilted her head. "Dropped off? What do you mean?"

"I mean that you seem in need of the comfort of your own sofa—and that back rub, pronto. So I'll drive you home and help you in and give these puppies a workout." He rubbed his hands together with a sweet smile. "I'll arrange to have your car driven to your place."

Okay, she was still on the fact that he'd said he was all in for that massage. But the car thing? "I'm not following, Theo. Why would you have my car dropped off? I'll just get a ride to the convention center in the morning."

"No worries," he said. "The ranch has runners who do odd jobs as needed. A nice tip and your car will be parked at your doorstep in a half hour."

Wow. Must be nice. "You definitely live in a different world than I do, Theo Abernathy. My dad's a truck driver. And my mother is part-time secretary. As I was growing up, we clipped coupons, watched our water usage, drove cars past the two-hundred-thousand-mile mark, and went on lake vacations every other summer for a long weekend. I've never left the country—heck, I've never been east of North Dakota."

He looked at her thoughtfully and nodded. "Well, now that we're friends and you're expecting a baby, I hope you'll let me spoil you a bit."

She bit her lip. She could use some spoiling. To a point, of course. Including that back rub.

"Well, I definitely don't think I can drive right now, so I'll take you up on that offer for a ride home. But I'll get my car myself tomorrow. Thank you, though. Old habits die hard, and I'm used to making arrangements for my own life."

"Gotcha," he said. He took her arm, the gallant gesture making her knees a little weak. "Your chariot awaits. My pickup truck, but it has very comfortable seats and a smooth ride, so that should help on the way home."

She inwardly sighed. Her eleven-year-old car made her feel every bump on the road.

As they made their way to the lot, his arm still entwined

with hers, she caught a few folks noticing. She could only imagine the speculation. *Is Theo the father of Bethany's baby? Are they dating?* It would be all over town in an hour.

Just friends, she'd tell anyone who asked her directly. Like her family and girlfriends.

Which was unfortunately the truth.

Chapter Nine

As they drove toward the apartment building in Bronco Valley, Bethany had to admit a gazillion-dollar pickup truck did have the smooth ride Theo had said it would. And excellent air-conditioning. He pulled into a spot in the small lot and hurried around to the passenger-side door to open it for her. As someone who traveled for wedding gigs in the band's guitarist's beat-up van with all their equipment, she wasn't used to anyone opening car doors for her—not that they should, of course. And she lugged equipment like everyone else. She tried to imagine Theo letting her lift a picnic cooler even if she wasn't pregnant. Ha—that would never happen.

Who wouldn't like a little doting? Especially when tired and hormonal. She smiled as he walked her to her door, feeling...cared for. Which helped her realize she really shouldn't let him upstairs for that back rub. That was just asking for trouble. He must know that.

But he had put himself at her service, anyway.

The man had a crush on the wedding singer with the voice he admired. She'd been there, experienced that. Men who liked that she was "artsy" and a free spirit—until she wanted more from them, like consistency, respect, and follow-through.

"I wonder who won the pet contest," Theo said as they stood on her doorstep, which was around the side of the hair salon.

"I hope that hairless cat, Lavinia," she said. "Anyone who'd adore that strange-looking creature deserves the win."

Theo laughed. "I think the chatty parrot named Goodie will win. He was my favorite. Especially when I said, 'Hi, Goodie,' and he said, 'Hi, Baddie.'"

Bethany grinned. "Clearly well trained by someone with a sense of humor." She bit her lip and avoided looking directly at Theo. She was afraid she'd grab his face and plant one on him. "I'll let you get going," she said. "Thanks for the ride."

"I promised you a back rub. And I've been told I give excellent massages," he added, holding up his hands.

Oh, by whom? she thought jealously.

That should have her making an excuse to get him to leave. Instead she unlocked the door and they went upstairs.

"My place isn't much, but it's cozy and serves its purpose," she said. "Depending on how far the wedding venue is that my band performs at and how late the reception goes, we often have comped rooms at a local hotel, so I'm really only here half the time."

As she huffed up the narrow, steep stairwell, she wondered how she'd navigate this at six months along, let alone nine months. And how she'd carry up a baby *and* a stroller. She hadn't really considered that when she'd first rented this place. Something to add to her long to-do list: check out affordable two-bedroom first-floor apartments.

Bethany opened the door to her apartment and immediately wondered what Theo would think. She liked the place a lot; whenever she came home, she always felt cheered by the bright, cozy space with her funky thrift-store treasures—the emerald green velvet sofa, the Persian rug, the gauzy curtains that warmed up the large windows. Her bedroom was her sanctuary and also thrift store decorated—the wrought iron bed and big fluffy rug that had cost more to have cleaned than to purchase.

She gave him a very quick tour, pointing out the galley kitchen, the tiny bathroom, her bedroom and the small guest room that would serve as a nursery. Hopefully she'd find a more suitable home before she started looking for a secondhand crib in excellent condition and a changing table.

"Nice place," Theo said, looking around. "I like your eclectic taste." He picked up a photo of the band on the faux fireplace mantel. "I recognize everyone, I think. I've been to several weddings that you and your band performed at."

Little did he know that her baby's father was in that photo. She'd almost replaced that picture with a newer one that didn't include Rexx, since he hadn't been in the band for a few months now. But something had always stopped her. He, like herself and the other three guys, were the original members and had been together for years. Plus, it kept Rexx in her life, even through just the sight of him in the photo, and she felt that was meaningful for her baby. She was going to try calling him again in the coming days to let him know she was pregnant, but she had no idea how that would go, what he'd say, what he'd want to do.

"I thought Bethany and the Belters were a foursome," Theo said, looking at the photo. "There are five here."

She swallowed. If only they'd hired a new bassist, he wouldn't have noticed. For now, the band was using a synthesizer until they found a replacement for Rexx.

She could feel herself about to blurt out a fact and went back and forth about it. *Just say it.* "The curly-haired blond on bass—that's Rexx. He's the baby's father."

His gaze darted to hers, then back to the photo. "Ah. You said he wasn't in the picture—though he literally is." He rolled his eyes at himself and held up a hand. "Forget I said that, since it almost sounded like a joke and I'm not making light of anything. He quit the band when you told him you were pregnant?"

She let out a breath. "Got time for a story?"

"I've got all night."

It was quite a story, though, and now she wasn't sure she wanted to tell him. It seemed so complicated. Theo would certainly find out how much being a mother meant to her, that she'd been about to get pregnant on purpose before she'd discovered a one-night stand had beat her to it. That was important for him to know, given how he felt about parenthood for himself.

She needed a little time to think and glanced at her phone, which she'd set on the coffee table. Just after 6:00 p.m. Dinnertime. "I could pop a frozen roasted-veggie pizza in the oven if you're getting hungry." It had been a few hours since they'd had those tacos, and now that she'd brought up the pizza, she was craving it.

"Sounds great," he said.

First lunch, now dinner. And making Theo dinner, even heating up a frozen pizza, seemed kind of…intimate.

Then again, it was just frozen pizza. Very casual. Something friends would share.

That made her feel better. Until she realized she'd also be sharing very personal details about herself and the pregnancy. Her friendship with Theo was only one day old. She'd feel even closer to him after telling him everything. That wasn't good.

She needed a little time to think. "Make yourself comfortable and I'll be right back," she told him, needing to flee into the kitchen.

"Better yet," he said, "*you* make yourself comfortable, and *I'll* take care of the pizza. Really—go sit, relax, put your feet up. Pizza and a back rub on the way."

She sucked in a breath. She'd long stopped believing in Prince Charming and knights in shining armor. But here was Theo Abernathy, surprising the hell out of her.

Again, this wasn't good.

"You sure?" she asked, needing to sit down as much as she needed a little space from this man. "It's really no trouble. Opening and shutting the oven, setting the timer."

"Therefore, I can do it. Sit," he said again with a smile.

Yes, sir, she thought wistfully. She'd have her space to think—and a soft seat.

She sat.

He put the photo of the band back, then turned to head into the kitchen.

She glanced at the pictures of her family, instantly comforted. Her parents. Her brother. The McCreerys all together. Soon she'd have the prints she'd ordered of the photos she'd taken at Jake and Elizabeth's wedding, including a really special one of the five kids in their wedding finery making funny faces. All her relatives had asked for a copy of that one, and her mom had said she planned to have it blown up poster size.

Bethany heard Theo opening the freezer, then the oven door opening and closing. Theo Abernathy was in her kitchen. Making her dinner.

Now *that* seemed very romantic. Very intimate.

She heard drawers and cabinet doors opening and closing, the clink of plates on the counter. Was he humming a song? The one she'd sung at his sister's surprise wedding the other day? She strained to listen.

He definitely was. She smiled, her heart soaring.

The man liked her—*that way*—there was no doubt about that. He was pursuing her whether he knew it or not. Whether he called it friendship or not. Maybe she could just go with that, see what happened. She could get hurt and probably would, but she was willing to see where this thing with Theo went. Maybe that same mentality for him meant he was changing before her eyes. Before his own eyes. It was possible.

"What can I bring you to drink?" he called out. "I'm looking in your fridge, and you have a pitcher of what I think is iced tea, three bottles of ginger ale, orange juice, and a lot of water."

"I'd love a ginger ale," she said. He sure was comfortable in her home. In her kitchen.

In moments, he'd brought her ginger ale in a glass with a few ice cubes. The delicious aroma of the pizza was starting to fill the air.

"Just a few more minutes on the pizza," he said. "How's that back doing?"

"Actually, it's better," she said quickly. If he put one finger on her body, she would melt in a puddle on the floor. And besides, she was so hyperfocused on him that she wasn't paying attention to her aches and pains and fatigue. She was both tired *and* wide-awake.

He sat on the arm on the sofa. Was it her imagination, or was his gaze on her belly, which had a slight rise?

"Has the baby kicked again?" he asked.

She couldn't have been more surprised. "Just a few more times. I love every flutter."

"Does it hurt?" he asked, wincing a bit.

She smiled. "Not really. It's just super exciting. That's my baby in there. My future."

He nodded thoughtfully. And seemed relieved when the oven timer dinged, because he popped up very quickly. "Back in a sec."

A few minutes later, he reappeared with the pizza cut into four slices on a round serving tray. He set that on the coffee table, then went back in the kitchen and returned with two plates and napkins, his own glass of ginger ale balanced on the plates. She could get used to this.

"We could move to the table if you prefer," he said, gesturing at the little round table by the window.

"I couldn't get up if I wanted," she said. And the table was way too romantic with its candlestick, even unlit, and view of the mountains in the distance.

"Sofa, it is, then," he said, sitting beside her. A few feet away but still close enough that she could smell the clean, masculine scent of him. Another sign she was hyperfocused on him, because the delicious aroma of the pizza had infused the air.

He set a slice on her plate and folded a napkin beside it. She had not expected a wealthy rancher who lived in a cabin-mansion and had "odd-job runners" at his disposal to be so domesticated.

"Bon appétit," he said, raising his glass to her.

She clinked her glass with his. "Bon appétit."

They ate and drank and talked about the day, the adorable pets they'd seen, his hilarious names for the dogs who'd walked by, and how he'd seen those lovebirds Winona and Stanley stealing a kiss by the cat section.

"I did too!" she said with a smile. "I'll be performing at their wedding. I can't wait to watch them say their I dos."

"Same here. They've both been through so much and deserve all the happiness in the world. When Robin invited Dylan to the Bonnie B for dinner to meet the family, he'd mentioned that his great-uncle had been widowed a few years ago after many decades of marriage. Stanley came to the US from Mexico soon after because he was so lonely. And then fell head over heels for an older woman." He smiled. "Winona's in her mid-*nineties*."

"I love their love story," Bethany said. "I know just a little about Winona's past. That she was reunited just a few years back with the daughter she'd had to give up for adoption as a teenager."

Theo took a sip of his ginger ale and nodded. "Such a sad story. At seventeen, Winona was madly in love with a boy her age named Josiah Abernathy—my great-grandfather. But when she got pregnant, her parents sent her away to a home for unwed mothers. Josiah was kept away from her by both sets of parents. He and Winona were told the baby died, but Josiah found out later that their baby was alive and had been adopted. By then, he'd been unable to find Winona. But he'd vowed to find their child."

Bethany felt her eyes widen. *My goodness.* What Winona and Josiah had gone through. "How did Winona and her daughter reunite? And what became of Josiah?"

Theo swallowed his bite of pizza. "A few years ago, Winona told her story to a new friend back in Rush Creek Falls. Melanie was determined to help Winona find her lost love. That led Melanie to Bronco and to the Flying A, where my aunt, uncle and cousins live. Melanie learned that Josiah was in a nursing home and suffering from Alzheimer's. But in a moment of lucidity, he'd told Melanie and his great-grandson Gabe Abernathy, my cousin, what he knew. That the baby was alive. Josiah soon passed away. Between Melanie and Gabe and a lot of help from people in Rust Creek Falls and Bronco, Winona was reunited with her long-lost daughter, Beatrix, now known as Daisy. They live together now."

"Such a happy ending for Winona. And a new love too."

Theo nodded. "Melanie and Gabe are married now. Winona ended up bringing a lot of couples together."

"Winona's been through so much that it's no wonder she got cold feet about marrying Stanley these past months," Bethany said. "But now, she's ready to say I do." She felt her eyes get misty and waved a hand. "I'm a softy. If we're going to be friends, you'll have to deal with that. I cry over emotional commercials too."

He smiled. "No problem. That's what tissues are for. And a strong shoulder," he added, raising his right one at her.

She laughed. "Watch out, I may take advantage."

"Go ahead," he said—very seriously. He added a warm smile, but it was too late. He'd already told her loud and clear that she could count on him.

Oh, boy. This really was getting dangerous. He was too wonderful.

"I was worried when it seemed like Winona and Stanley were headed for a breakup," Theo said. "But you can see how in love they are when they're together. Even *I'm* a softy when I see them around town."

"I've been through so many breakups myself," Bethany said, "but not once have I gotten back together with anyone. It's how I know none of my exes was the 'one who got away.'"

"Me either. Speaking of exes," he added, "have you and Rexx figured out how you're going to coparent?"

Bethany swallowed and put down her pizza, glad she'd eaten practically the whole slice already, because her appetite had now vanished. "He doesn't even know I'm pregnant."

The whole story poured out. That she'd never been particularly attracted to Rexx and they had little in common or chemistry, but they'd been at a hotel after a late-night wedding gig and had found themselves in the bar, drinking to how love had passed them both by. One drink too many, and they'd woken up at the crack of dawn in her room. Naked. That they'd both been embarrassed—and both had been grateful to see the empty condom wrapper on the floor. At least they'd been responsible.

Too bad the condom hadn't been. They hadn't known it at the time, of course, but it must have torn.

She told Theo how she and Rexx had decided for the sake of the band to forget that this had ever happened and go about their merry ways. "But in the following days, I thought, *maybe this is why I'm single. Because I keep moving away from potential love. Who's to say Rexx and I wouldn't work out? Maybe we have more in common than I think. I should give this a chance. I'm thirty-five, not twenty-five.*"

"I had that conversation with myself after some of my recent dates. But when you're forcing it, you're forcing it."

Bethany nodded. "Exactly. And thank the heavens that before I could share my epiphany with him, he announced that he was quitting the band, that he'd fallen for a bridesmaid at a wedding we'd performed at days later, and when you know, you know, sorry, bye."

"Ow," Theo said. "That still must have been hard on you."

"Well, it was really more a wake-up call. That I was willing to date someone I didn't have any chemistry with because love did seem to have passed me by and my biological clock was ticking and I wanted a child. So I realized enough was enough—that I was going to pursue in vitro fertilization and single motherhood. That I'd make my dream come true myself."

Theo's eyes narrowed. "Okay, now I'm confused."

Bethany smiled. "I had already been researching my options before I slept with Rexx. After that night, I realized I wanted to try to have a baby on my own, so I made my appointment at the fertility center, and after some testing, the doctor said, 'Congratulations—you're *already* pregnant.'"

"Ah," Theo said. "Wow."

"Yup." She told him the rest, how she'd called Rexx to tell him but he'd cut her off before she could share the news. "He's engaged to that bridesmaid and wants no contact with any exes. Not that I qualify as an ex. I'm planning to call him this week to tell him. It's wrong to keep it from him."

"Well, if you need that shoulder," he said, lifting it again, "I'm here for you, okay?"

She smiled shakily, because she could easily burst into tears. "Okay."

Despite what he'd just said, she still expected him to bolt out the door. Not only was she pregnant, but things were a bit complicated.

She gave him a minute to make an excuse to leave. He was done with his pizza and the ginger ale.

And he now knew just how far she'd been willing to go to have a baby.

But he didn't move. He just reached for her hand and held it.

And right there, Bethany felt herself falling hard for this man.

Chapter Ten

Theo was having a hard time understanding himself at the moment. He was sitting here on Bethany's sofa, holding her hand. And desperately wanting to kiss her.

Not a sweet peck on the cheek.

Not a friendly lips to the forehead.

A long, slow, passionate kiss on the lips.

He'd wanted to kiss her all day. And now that she'd opened up to him, he was feeling even closer to her. But it wasn't their new friendship that had him feeling so warmly toward her.

It was red-hot attraction. Chemistry. An awareness that she was under his skin in a way no woman had ever been. And he'd had plenty of girlfriends.

He kept trying to remind himself that she was pregnant, that she was a package deal, that kissing her was out of the question.

But all he could think about at the moment was holding her. Touching her. Feeling her in his arms.

What the heck was wrong with him?

He didn't suddenly want to be a father in five months. He didn't suddenly feel ready to have a family.

Do. Not. Give. This. Woman. Mixed. Signals. He said it to himself three times so that it would get through his clearly befuddled head. It was one thing for him to be confused about what the hell was going on with him. It was another to confuse Bethany. She had enough on her plate. Enough to worry about.

No kiss. Period.

Instead, help her out, he told himself. *Be there for her in the ways you can be.* On the tour of her apartment, he'd noticed there were very few baby items—a big stuffed rabbit, a pair of pj's, but not any necessities, like a crib or even a bassinet. He could easily outfit her spare bedroom into a nursery with everything she'd need. Everything a baby would need. Jace could help him with that. So could Google.

He could also offer Bethany one of the spare guest cabins at the Bonnie B, two of which had two bedrooms. The furnished cabins were bigger than her apartment—and one story, no stairs for her to try to huff up when she was nine months pregnant.

Maybe he was getting ahead of himself. They'd just become friends. But the ranch *did* have the spare cabins, and she'd be much more comfortable. What were friends for if not to help out? Especially when it was easy-peasy.

He could just see his siblings' faces if he told them that Bethany would be moving into a guest cabin until she was ready to find a new place—probably not until the baby was six months old and she was more settled into motherhood. He could hear Jace now: *You sure do seem to care about this woman. This pregnant woman.*

He inwardly sighed. He had it right the first time—he was getting ahead of himself. In fact, he should get going. But again, he couldn't seem to stand up. Or leave this woman's side.

"What do you think Rexx will say when you tell him about the baby?" he said instead of walking out the door. Because he *did* care about Bethany. And what her immediate future held. Would she be on her own financially? On her own, period?

"Honestly, I don't know," she said. "I always thought of him as a decent guy, but he's about to get a bombshell dropped on him when he's engaged to be married. Will he suddenly say it's a bad connection and end the call? Will he say, 'Well, let's sit down and figure out how we can coparent'?" She bit her lip and seemed worried. "What a mess." She sat back against the sofa. "Everything is just so…unknown. Up in the air."

"Except for how happy you are that you're gonna be a mama," he said. Where *that* little burst of optimism had come from, he wasn't sure. He only knew he wanted to make Bethany McCreery feel better, smile.

She seemed so touched—to the point that she leaned forward as though to kiss him on the cheek. But in the same moment, he leaned forward. And his lips landed on her lips.

Once there, he couldn't make himself pull away.

She didn't either.

He inched closer, deepening the kiss. He reached up to cup her face with his hand. He felt her arms go around his neck. He moved even closer. Slipped his tongue inside her soft, warm mouth.

Mmm, he could do this forever, the sweet anticipation of more to come sending goose bumps up his spine.

Until she pulled away. He opened his eyes to see her not frowning, exactly, but hardly smiling.

"I think we both forgot for a second that we're not a love match," she said. She patted her belly.

"Actually, the fact that you're pregnant is always on my mind, Bethany."

She tilted her head. "Meaning?"

"Meaning…" What did he mean? He sighed again. "To be honest, I don't know." He smiled and threw up his hands. "I'm usually very easy to figure out. Just ask my siblings."

"I think I know what you meant," she said. "You're interested in me as more than a friend, but I *am* pregnant and you can't forget that, so friends it is."

"Except we kissed. Definitely something friends don't do." He stood up and gathered their plates and glasses. "I guess I'd better get going." He paused and set the plates and glasses back down. "I almost forgot I promised you a back rub."

He really was out of his mind for bringing that up. But he had promised her. And Theo Abernathy kept his promises even when they were inconvenient.

Her eyes widened. "I guess back rubs are in the friend zone. I mean, my brother gave me a back rub the other day."

Still. Why the heck had he reminded her? He couldn't possibly touch her. Not after that kiss.

"Okay, sure," she said, as if settling something for herself. "There's just one spot that aches if I move wrong." She reached behind her to give the area a squeeze.

Just keep control, he told himself. He sucked in a quick breath. "Let me at it."

She laughed and turned slightly, giving a spot above her left hip a tap. "If you get rid of this knot, you'll be my hero."

I'd like to be your hero, he thought. *But that's the last thing I am where you're concerned.*

The moment his hand touched the fabric of her dress against her body, he felt electric pulses run along his nerve endings. He used both hands on her knot, careful not to rub or squeeze too hard. He wanted to take her in his arms and hold her—just hold her—so that everything in his jumbled head would make sense. Because when it was just the two of them, talking, sharing, opening up to each other, he felt as though he had everything he'd ever need.

This woman was starting to mean so much to him. No matter how hard he tried to step back, he couldn't. And touching her was taking him two steps forward.

He gently pressed into her soft skin, wanting to drop a kiss on the knot he was undoing. He loved her *aahs*, the little moans of pleasure making him wonder what she'd sound like if his hands roamed much lower…

"Oh, Theo, you're as good as you said. This feels amazing. You definitely made the knot much looser."

He was actually relieved to be able to remove his hands from her body. He wanted to touch every inch of her. Which meant he had to leave. Now.

He stood again, collected their dishware again.

"Thanks for everything today—and tonight," she said. "I had a great time."

He looked at her, beautiful Bethany. Pregnant Bethany.

"Me too," he said fast and practically ran into the kitchen. He placed the dishes and glasses in her dishwasher, adding the pizza cutter from the sink. He stared out the window to give himself a moment—to forget the kiss. To forget massaging her. To remember *himself*—that he was not ready for the life Bethany would have in five months.

Okay, time to go, he ordered himself. *You don't belong here. The two of you are* not *a match of* any *kind.*

With that clear in his jumbled brain, he went back to the living room. "See you," he said, taking his Stetson from the bottom tier of the coffee table and dropping it on his head. The *See you* was so stupid that he frowned and didn't move. *The door is that way*, he told himself. *So go already.*

He still didn't move.

Bethany stood. "It's okay, Theo. We are who we are, right? I want a baby—so much that I was going to make it happen through the wonders of science and test tubes. You want to live on your own terms—not via a baby's needs and schedule. No one's wrong here."

Except that I don't get to have you, then, he wanted to say.

But didn't.

"Maybe we can meet for coffee soon," he said—another inept goodbye.

Coffee. When he wanted to set her up in a guest cabin at the Bonnie B. Outfit the second bedroom as a deluxe nursery with everything she and her baby could possibly need. When he wanted to rub her back again. Kiss her again.

"I'd like that," she said with a warm smile. Which he knew hid how she really felt. That she likely wished he wasn't so...what? Stubborn. It wasn't so much living on his own terms that had put him off fatherhood; it was more his responsibilities to the ranch, to his family. To the podcast he so loved using so much of his spare time for. But his brothers cared about the Bonnie B just as much as he did, and they'd figured it out. Billy with his three teens and a pregnant fiancée, and Jace with a one-year-old and a fiancée of his own, weren't any less there for the ranch than he was.

So what was going on with him, *really*?

Theo gave her a tight smile and headed to the door. Pulling it open took just about everything out of him.

So did leaving.

The next morning, Bethany sat at her kitchen table and texted back her bandmate Harry, the guitarist, to confirm their rehearsal later this morning. She wanted to make sure all the songs they'd perform at Winona and Stanley's wedding were perfect, and they barely had two weeks. Plus the band needed to work on three additional songs for their two gigs this weekend. Just when Bethany thought she knew every love song out there, a bride or groom threw her a surprise ballad.

Between thinking about the band and the word *surprise*, Rexx came to mind. And her assurance to her mother and herself that she'd call him with the news.

She stared at her phone, which was beside her mug of steaming chamomile tea, whole wheat toast with strawberry jam, and the book she toted around everywhere these days—these months—*Your Pregnancy Month by Month*.

Call Rexx, she told herself. *Just do it*.

It wasn't yet nine o'clock, though. She'd wait till nine, which seemed a reasonable hour to call someone who wasn't family or a bestie.

How about the unwitting father of your child?

She wrapped her hands around the mug, breathing in the comforting aroma of the chamomile. She took a sip and turned to the bookmarked page in *Your Pregnancy*

Month by Month. This week focused on digestive problems, breast changes, stretch marks, and vivid dreams.

Bethany was grateful she couldn't concentrate on what she was reading. She didn't want to think about heartburn and how she was going to need new bras in a bigger size—another expense. Not to mention that more stretch marks were coming her way, since she had a few already. But she didn't want to keep thinking about Theo either. The kiss. And his awkward exit, not just from her apartment but clearly from her life.

Maybe we can meet for coffee soon...

That was definitely a goodbye.

She'd barely gotten any sleep because of that goodbye. And the kiss. And the way he'd doted on her all day and evening.

Actually, the fact that you're pregnant is always on my mind...

A man who felt the way he did, who'd been up front about it, should have run when he found out she was pregnant. Instead, he was taking care of dinner and bringing her ginger ale. Rubbing her achy back.

Kissing her passionately on the lips.

Could he change his mind? Was that actually possible? Whenever Bethany used to tell her late grandmother about her bad dates, Gram would call up one of her favorite sayings: *When people show you who they are, believe them the first time.*

That was why Bethany hadn't written him off. He kept showing her that he was a kind, warm, caring person who'd make an excellent father.

Poor Theo. He said one thing, but his actions shouted something else.

She hadn't been surprised that she'd dreamed about him last night—as intensely and vividly as the pregnancy book told her to expect. She and Theo had been at his family ranch, but the Bonnie B had turned into a baby store that went on for acres. His sister Robin and her new groom, Dylan Sanchez, were riding together on a white horse up and down the aisles. Theo was holding a little green onesie with Big Sky Baby written across the chest. *We'll take a thousand of these*, he'd told the horse, who was for some reason doubling as the store clerk.

She'd woken up as he'd been putting onesie after onesie in the horse's saddlebag. Where the newlyweds had gone, she had no idea. Maybe if she hadn't woken up, she and Theo would have gotten on that horse and ridden off into the sunset together.

He *could* change his mind about being a father in the very near future.

But if he didn't, and she let herself fall for him…

She took a sip of her tea and glanced at her phone— 9:01. Time to call Rexx.

Butterflies flew around her stomach, and she shoved aside the toast and took another few sips of her herbal tea. No caffeine boost there, unfortunately.

Just do it. Bethany picked up her phone and slid through her contacts until she got to Rexx. She was about to press the Call icon next to his name, but she needed a second. She sucked in a breath, bracing herself to hear his raspy voice saying, *Bethany, I told you—I don't want contact with my old life.*

Problem with that was that they'd created a *new* life.

Okay. Here goes. She pressed the little phone icon next to Rexx's name.

But instead of his annoyed voice, she heard an automated message: "The number you have reached, 406-555-2522, is no longer in service."

She gasped. He'd changed his number.

She hadn't expected that at all. But she probably should have.

Rexx really didn't want anything to do with her. She was the last woman he'd been with before he'd fallen hard for his fiancée, and the new lady in his life was clearly the jealous type and had insisted he cut off contact with anyone from his life before her. After all, he'd gone as far as to quit the band, which was a big deal given that they were reasonably successful and got along well.

Granted, she doubted it had entered his mind that the reason she'd call him was because she was pregnant. They *had* used a condom. It just hadn't done its job, and Rexx clearly hadn't noticed the tear.

Now what? Did she respect how he felt when she had something monumental to tell him? How could she? He deserved to know—no matter what. Just as her baby deserved for Bethany to make the effort.

Maybe one of the band members had Rexx's new number.

Then again, he'd been so quick to walk away from the band that he likely had cut them all out of his life. She'd find out at today's rehearsal.

She sighed for tenth time that morning and reached for her book. Reading about stretch marks and heartburn couldn't be worse than how up in the air she felt.

After two cattle auctions this morning, Theo was on his way back to the ranch when he was about to pass Hey, Baby, where everyone in town, including himself, bought their little relatives birthday gifts. When his brother and soon-to-be sister-in-law Charlotte announced they were expecting, he'd popped into Hey, Baby for a gift, the saleswoman giving him five good ideas for what to buy. He could stop in and pick up a few things for Bethany's nursery since he was right here. He slowed down and turned into the parking lot.

Theo hadn't spoken to Bethany since he'd left her apartment last night. Three times he'd pulled out his phone to shoot off a quick text, just something casual and friendly to get them both away from the awkward way they'd left things.

See you, he'd told her as he'd left her apartment, as though she was an acquaintance he'd run into in the grocery store. And then he'd said something inane about meeting up for coffee sometime.

Last night, when he'd tried to sleep, he'd replayed their night together over and over. How much he liked her. How attracted he was to her. The way he'd fussed over her—making the pizza, serving it, rubbing her back.

Kissing her.

And if she hadn't put an end to that kiss? What if it had led them into her bedroom?

We are who we are, right? I want a baby—so much that I was going to make it happen through the wonders of science and test tubes. You want to live on your own terms—not via a baby's needs and schedule. No one's wrong here.

Her words echoing in his head, he parked and went inside the store. He pulled out his phone to consult the "nursery essentials" lists he'd bookmarked just as a couple with a stroller entered the shop—arguing.

"No, you can't go to Ethan's bachelor party," the woman said. "Stop trying to get me to change my mind."

The man threw up his hands. "It's one night, Lizzie. Jeez."

Theo literally saw the woman's hands blanch on the handle of the stroller, her gold wedding ring glinting. She turned to the guy. "Well, we have a baby and a sick toddler at home, and neither of our families can help me tonight. How could you even *want* to go?"

"It's a few hours," the man whined.

Theo couldn't help but notice the guy was twisting his own gold wedding ring on his finger.

"More like seven or eight hours, and then you'll come home drunk," the woman said with more exasperation than anger in her voice. "Lot of help you'll be with Danny's 3:00 a.m. feeding. You'd probably drop him."

The man sighed. The woman shook her head. "Fine, I won't go. Happy?"

It was clear to Theo they'd had a version of this conversation a million times. "No, actually. I'm not. I want you to *care*."

The man put his arms around his wife and tilted up her chin. "I do care. Of course I care."

Theo had heard enough. He did a literal 180 and headed for the door. He suddenly had little interest in shopping for cribs or bouncy seats or any of the other baby essentials he'd researched during his morning coffee. His search had led him to a bunch of baby shower registration lists, and there were countless items, from smart bassinets that you could set to rock or play a lullaby with a tap on your phone's app to a wipe warmer so that baby's tiny tush didn't get startled by a cold touch during a diaper change.

He'd learned quite a bit from the registry lists. He could create a top-of-the-line nursery for Bethany with a few clicks of his keyboard, but he'd wanted to see some of the big-ticket items for himself, make sure the quality was there.

It hadn't been lost on him that he had been researching all that stuff. But he'd figured he was doing it because Bethany was on her own and money was tight.

But he suddenly felt a little queasy.

He would never be like that dad, more concerned with a fun night out than with his responsibilities at home. His sick toddler needed him. His wife needed him. Theo's heart would have him at home, so he and his future wife would never have a conversation like that.

But, but, but… How could Theo be there for his wife and child—*children*—if he was on the range or the barn, giving one hundred percent to the Bonnie B? The ranch was his world. And maybe because his brothers *did* have responsibility to their own families, Theo felt it was *his* responsibility to step in when they were needed elsewhere— at home with a sick kid or at a parent-teacher conference, or cheering from the stands at a school game. He couldn't be pulled in different directions. Period. Maybe in a few years he'd feel the tug of fatherhood. But he wasn't anywhere close to that.

The key was not to do something you weren't truly ready for.

Which meant keeping his friendship with Bethany squarely in the friend zone. No more kissing.

With that settled, he turned back around—ready to shop. Friends could definitely help out new-mother-to-be friends with a few necessities.

But as he studied the bassinets and consulted the registry lists he'd saved, he realized he was putting a lot more time and energy into Bethany's baby than he had for his nephew Frankie over the past year. He'd practically bought out the internet for Frankie once it was clear that Jace would adopt the baby. So had his siblings, and since they hadn't coordinated, Jace and Tamara had ended up with three bouncy seats, four baby bathtubs, four strollers, and so many huge stuffed animals that they didn't fit in the large nursery. Theo had just pointed and clicked then; he hadn't studied the reviews the way he was doing now, only considering a baby monitor with five stars and more than one hundred positive write-ups.

As he tried on a model of a top-of-the-line infant carrier, spending a good twenty minutes figuring out how the contraption buckled onto his chest and testing its security, Theo was once again left wondering what was going on.

His phone pinged with a text.

Hey, bro. Up for babysitting Frankie tomorrow night? 6:30 to 9ish. Something came up last minute and you're my only hope.

Uh oh. Two and a half hours on his own with a baby? He loved his nephew and Frankie was an easy baby who'd be asleep most of that time, but hadn't Jace mentioned that Frankie was teething and woke up cranky a couple times a night? Theo had been planning on recording the introduction for next week's episode of *This Ranching Life* tomorrow night, and now he'd have to put it off. He had little free time as it was.

But given how he couldn't get Bethany off his mind and

the fact that he was here in Hey, Baby with a carrier on his chest, babysitting Frankie was exactly what he needed to do.

Tomorrow night would reinforce that he wasn't ready to be anyone's dad. Theo instantly brightened. Yes. That was exactly what he needed. To have his truth brought home for him.

Plus, if Theo was his brother's last hope, that meant he'd asked everyone else and no one was available. He texted Jace a yes. It was a win-win for both of them.

Chapter Eleven

Bethany had a lot on her mind when she finally pulled into her apartment building's parking lot after a long but good rehearsal with the band. Including the fact that none of the guys had Rexx's new number. The drummer and keyboardist had said they wouldn't care if they ever heard from that "jerk" again after the way he'd left them high and dry without a bassist, but the guitarist, who was also their backup vocalist, had never liked Rexx anyway and insisted they were fine without one. The way Bethany saw it, splitting the money by four instead of five made a huge difference.

When she explained to the band why she needed to talk to Rexx, they were all full of congratulations and hugs and they'd come up with a hand gesture Bethany could give during a gig if she was ever feeling sick or tired and needed to dash off suddenly for a bit. They'd all quickly cover for her. They were such great guys.

The drummer had suggested getting in touch with the bride at whose wedding Rexx had met his fiancée to get *her* contact info. Hmm, Bethany couldn't see doing that. *Um, hi, could you give me your fiancé's cell number even though he changed it to avoid hearing from me? I need to tell him I'm pregnant with his child.*

She sighed and got out of her car. She wasn't giving up on getting in touch with Rexx, but she was exhausted and done thinking for the day. What she wanted now was to make some popcorn, watch a rom-com, and then practice the two ballads that had a couple of tricky high notes. That should keep her mind occupied so she wouldn't think about Theo. She'd been failing at that all day. The good news was that she hadn't heard from him. *Good* because they really couldn't be friends. And the fact that she'd been disappointed by not getting a call or text from him made that very clear. Her heart was already involved, and she had to put the kibosh on that.

She opened the front door, surprised to see a stack of packages both big and small from Hey, Baby—her favorite shop to explore, if not buy from since it was on the pricey side—piled high on the side of the stairwell. Huh. There were only two apartments, hers and the young single cowboy who lived on the third floor. He was definitely home since she heard his loud country-western music from down here, but wouldn't he have brought up his deliveries already?

She eyed the name on the top package. Bethany Mc-Creery. What was this? A mistake? She hadn't ordered anything in weeks. All the packages—five of them—had her name and address. She opened the top one and pulled out a pair of adorable silver baby booties embroidered with tiny stars. Someone had sent her a baby gift? Five baby gifts, including two that were very large? She slid out the packing label. The billing name and address were Theo Abernathy's.

What was going on?

She took out her phone and called him. He answered right away.

"Theo, there are five packages of varying sizes in my tiny lobby," she said. "I opened one and it's from you. Really cute baby booties."

"Oh, good," he said. "Everything arrived. I'll come over and bring them up for you. I can put everything together too."

Um, the whole point of the popcorn and rom-com was to relax and busy herself so she wouldn't think about him. Now he was coming over? "Wait—put *what* together?"

"I wanted to surprise you with a few things for the baby's nursery. The store had a same-day delivery option and my truck was packed with some ranch equipment I bought today, so I opted for that."

She stared at the boxes. The bottom two were quite big. What the heck was in there? "Theo, you didn't need to buy me anything."

"I wanted to," he said. "I'm very handy with an Allen wrench too. See you in a few?"

"Okay," she said. She was confused. First he was doting on her. Now he was buying out Hey, Baby. What was he doing? They were new friends, and new friends didn't do this. Old friends didn't do this. Baby booties, sure. But there were *five* packages here.

They also didn't show up with Allen wrenches to put together a crib or a high chair.

And when had he bought all this stuff? Today at some point. Which meant he'd been thinking about her. And had spent quite a bit of time making choices and purchases. He had to be working out his feelings for her, for the pregnant woman he was unexpectedly interested in. But just as she'd thought earlier, as he worked it out by spending time with her, by buying silver baby booties, by making her feel special and desirable, she was being left to fall for him.

And when he decided that he'd been right to begin with, that he *wasn't* ready, that he didn't want this, she'd be left with a bruised heart.

With a baby to care for. She'd be exhausted and stressed enough as a brand-new mother; she wasn't adding sad and confused to the mix. Her baby deserved better than that.

She stared at the packages and shook her head. Theo would have to take all this back. That was the end of it.

Bethany sat down on the third step, since that would be the easiest to get up from, and waited. She played a word game on her phone, trying to keep her irritation at bay. Theo clearly meant well. But working out his confusion at her expense, whether he knew what he was doing or not, was a big problem.

She saw him pulling in. Dammit. She should have told him to bring a truck because he was taking all this back.

He saw her through the glass on the door and smiled, then came inside. He held what looked like a toolbox.

She got herself up. "Theo, whatever all this is, I appreciate it. But I want you to take it back. I can't accept it."

His face fell. "I hope you can, Bethany. I noticed you didn't have anything set up for the baby's nursery yet. And you mentioned that money was tight, so…"

She frowned and lifted her chin. She had no doubt that he'd spent a small fortune without having to think twice or even look at price tags. "Theo Abernathy, I've always supported myself, and I'll support my baby just fine on my own."

He seemed at a loss for words. "I know, and I admire

you, Bethany. To be honest, I was about to pass the store, but then I thought of you and went in. Between Frankie's nursery and my research, I knew what you needed, so I... bought a few things."

"But why?" she asked.

He stared at her, flustered.

Now she felt bad. But this was a bit beyond.

"I want you to have what you need," he said. "That's all there is to it."

"Because I'm on my own?"

"First and foremost because you're my friend. And yes, the baby's father isn't in the picture. Does he know now that you're pregnant? Is he planning to step up?"

She sighed and told him about the call to Rexx, about the automated message. And that none of the other band members had his new contact info either.

He shook his head. "So let me help, Bethany. Because I very easily *can*."

He looked so sincere, his green eyes warm—and friendly. But she had to call him out on his privilege.

"Theo, I appreciate that you care—and your generosity. But where I come from, which is Bronco Valley, I budget for what I can afford, buy only what I need—and I work for it. That's how I live, okay?"

He was looking at her intently, his head slightly tilting as if he hadn't expected that, hadn't even considered that what he'd said was...privileged. *Stick around*, she thought. *You'll be down to earth in no time*. "Bethany," he said, "I hear you. I absolutely do. I can't apologize for having money. But I also can't think of a better thing to do with it than help my friend create the best possible home-sweet-home for her baby. I just want to do something nice for you."

Swoon. He always knew what to say. "You're a nice guy, Theo Abernathy."

He smiled. "Money can't buy that. I was made this way."

She laughed. "I'll take the light packages."

That handsome face brightened.

She scooped up the three small boxes, including the one with the booties, still unsure about all this, where this was headed, where *they* were headed. She had more to say, but she didn't want to talk out here in the open, even though the upstairs cowboy's music would make it impossible for the guy to eavesdrop. Nor would he be remotely interested in the conversation.

Theo took one of the big boxes, his toolbox atop it, and followed her up the stairs, set it down, then went back for the other one.

She opened her apartment door and held it open wide for him. Once they were inside and he was putting down a box in the living room, she couldn't keep her thoughts inside anymore.

"There's something else too," she said.

He sat on the edge of the sofa. "I'm listening."

He was looking at her so intently. She'd gone out with men who gazed around even while she talked about something important. Especially lately, she wasn't used to having such undivided attention. She liked it.

"I've been thinking about that kiss. And then after. How you left in a hurry. And then suddenly you're buying out the baby section and here in my apartment with your toolbox. It all makes me think you're playing out your feelings about me being pregnant."

He seemed a little confused by that. "I don't think so, Bethany. I told you why I got all this for you."

He probably was doing it all unconsciously. Just going with the moment. But that would have the same end result.

Bethany with a busted-up heart. Expectations set up and squashed. Hopes dashed.

"In the end, you're not going to be my boyfriend, Theo. You're not going to be a father figure in the baby's life. Which is fine—you've been very up front about that. The problem is that…"

He was waiting. And she felt close to tears. As if everything she'd been hoping for over the past year was right in front of her but still unattainable.

Out with it, Bethany.

"I'm afraid that this knight-in-shining-armor stuff is going to affect me too much. Know what I'm saying?"

It was clear that he didn't. But then his brows kind of knitted and he seemed flustered again. She saw when the light bulb went off in his head and he understood.

"I can't afford to get hurt, Theo. Not when I need to be preparing for motherhood."

Now he was looking at her thoughtfully, as though he was taking in everything she'd just said. "Right, so no more kissing. But are you saying we can't be friends?"

Was she? She supposed she was. But that wasn't what she wanted either.

"I don't know what I'm saying, Theo. That's why this is so hard."

"Yeah, same here. I mean, I had an answer about why I bought all this stuff. Why I'm here at all. But it doesn't really make sense, does it?"

She shook her head. She would just have to focus on the

word *friendship*. Friendship, friendship, friendship. There would be no more kissing. Theo Abernathy was like a new instant bestie. *Yeah, right*, she thought. This was just the beginning of a lot more to come and she knew it.

"Well, let me get everything put together," he said, opening the toolbox and holding up the Allen wrench. "I like assembling. It's easy when the directions come with labeled illustrations. Unlike..."

"Us," she finished for him.

He nodded and knelt down beside the box, getting out an X-Acto knife.

She sighed. "Theo. You're supposed to make yourself less desirable, not more. And the fact that I've got this baby bump, that these things are all baby stuff, should make *me* less desirable to you. Not more."

He smiled, and it went right inside her. "Like I said, we don't make sense. But here we are."

Yeah, and now what? But unless she told him to leave and take all the baby stuff with him, there would be a to-morrow and the next day and the next day. Before she knew it, he'd be coming to Lamaze class with her.

He patted the box. "This is probably the deluxe baby bouncer. It's a smart one. Tap a button on the app and it plays lullabies."

Oh, Theo, she thought for the millionth time since her brother's wedding.

What was she supposed to do about this man?

Theo pressed the button marked Gentle Play, and the pastel-colored mobile with its tiny dangling stuffed animals began spinning. "And my work here is done," he said with a smile. It had taken almost two hours to put everything together, but now he wished he had something else to assemble so he wouldn't have to leave.

He stood with Bethany in her spare bedroom, which was looking a lot like a nursery now. There was the bassinet across from the window with the cute mobile atop it, the smart bouncy seat, the changing table with a terry cloth–covered pad and three drawers underneath, the baby booties, and ten pairs of birth- to three-month-sized pajamas.

"Oh, Theo," she said, looking around the room, her hand over her heart, which touched him. "I love everything. Thank you."

"You're welcome. And the reason I opted for a bassinet and not a crib is just in case we don't have the same taste. They had very fancy ones and plain ones and everything in between and in all different colors—white and gray and light and dark wood."

Bethany smiled. "I have no idea what style I'd like. I guess I'd have to go to a baby store and look around to know my own taste. I'd think I'd like plain so I could stencil the baby's name on it, but who knows? Maybe I'd want some huge sleigh crib."

"Speaking of a huge sleigh crib," he said. "There are a couple of guest cabins at the Bonnie B with two bedrooms. You're welcome to move into one if you'd like. They're pretty roomy. A sleigh crib would fit with no problem."

He saw her bite her lip before she glanced away. Maybe he shouldn't have brought it up yet. Too much, too soon, probably. He was the king of that lately.

"That's some offer, Theo," she said.

"I just want you to be comfortable. I'm trying to imagine you getting up those steep stairs at nine months pregnant, and then carrying a newborn down with whatever else you might have to take with you. The guest cabins are one story. And they're a good distance from the main working areas of the ranch, so you won't be woken up by Buster crowing."

She laughed, but her smile faded some. "This apartment definitely isn't ideal. And yes, I'll probably need one of those chairlifts to get up here in a couple of months," she added on a half chuckle. "But… I don't know, Theo."

He nodded. "Just know the offer stands."

"I appreciate it."

He figured he'd better change the subject fast, because she looked uncomfortable. He was definitely going too far. Getting ahead of himself *and* going too far.

He showed her how to use the app on her phone to remotely operate the mobile. "According to the description, you could be in the kitchen making dinner and hear the baby fuss and just tap a button on your phone and voilà, the mobile will remotely spin and play a lullaby to keep Bethany Junior occupied, giving you a few minutes."

"Bethany Junior," she said, her beautiful face lighting up. "I like it."

"Have you thought about names?" he asked.

"Like everything else, no. I've barely bought anything for the baby either. Either it doesn't feel real that I'm going to be a mother in five months or I'm actually a little scared."

"Scared of what?"

She bit her lip again. "Well, I will be on my own. In the middle of the night, when it's time to feed a two-day-old baby, it'll be just me, you know? And I barely know anything. I was reading about how to care for the umbilical cord stump in the days after birth and got so nervous I had to close my pregnancy book." She let out a breath. "I had so much experience with babies when my niece and nephews were born, but the youngest is six now. I haven't picked up a baby in years."

His green eyes lit up. "If you're looking for a refresher course, I'm babysitting tomorrow night for my brother's son, Frankie. He's only twelve months old. And trust me when I say I could use your help."

She laughed. "Of course I'll help. Count me in. It's the least I can do after all this, Theo."

He held her gaze and couldn't drag his eyes off her if he wanted to. He was about to say something stupid like *that's what friends are for*, but he just sucked in a breath.

"Try out the mobile app," he said, needing to ruin the moment.

She pressed the button he'd pointed out, and looked almost astonished when the mobile began playing Brahms' lullaby. "Amazing, Theo. I love technology." She watched the little dangling animals spin around atop the bassinet, the lullaby playing softy.

She dabbed under her eyes. "I didn't think I'd get all emotional, but aww. This is real, you know? The baby will be here in five months. And now I have a nursery." She gazed around and looked so moved that he wanted to take her in his arms and just hold her.

But he wanted so much more than that. He wanted to feel her against him—her body, her mouth. He wanted to tell her she'd never want for anything with him in her life, that he'd always be there for her.

But how could he when he couldn't be the one thing she needed? A father for her child.

He reached for her hand and gave it a quick squeeze. "I just want you and the baby to have everything you need."

She looked at him, then quickly glanced away.

"Really, Theo, thank you for all this. Especially after the big...nothing from Rexx, the extreme of too much from you turned out to be just what I needed."

He smiled, feeling much better about his decision to get her nursery going. "I just want you to know that no matter what, I'm here for you."

"Friends," she said, sticking out her hand. "I think we need to be clear on that. Because like I said, I really can't risk getting hurt by you."

He had so much to say, but nothing would come out of his mouth. He couldn't imagine hurting her. But she was right to back off. As much as he cared about her, *wanted* her, he wasn't what she needed.

Finally he just nodded. "Friends." He shook, the feel of her warm, soft hand sending tingles along his nerve endings.

At the least, he wanted to add.

Theo could feel himself on a course for trouble here.

Chapter Twelve

The next afternoon, after another rehearsal with the band, Bethany had plans to meet her new sister-in-law, Elizabeth, for an early dinner at the Gemstone Diner. For once, it would be just the two of them. Usually they were surrounded by Elizabeth's five-year-old twins and Jake and his three kids, but finally they'd be able to have some much-needed girl talk. Elizabeth only had an hour before she'd be meeting her sisters for their own practice for an upcoming rodeo out of town, and Bethany would be meeting Theo at his cabin at six for their night of babysitting.

When she pulled open the door, she immediately saw Elizabeth because there was a small crowd around her table. That was life for the Hawkins Sisters—they were superstars in the rodeo community, and since Elizabeth, some of her sisters and several of her cousins had married Bronco residents, they were now hometown celebrities.

As Bethany approached the table, the crowd dispersed. Elizabeth stood and gave Bethany a warm hug.

"How's married life?" Bethany asked as they sat down.

Elizabeth's face lit up. "I love it. I love your brother to pieces. And the kids are getting along beautifully." She sighed. "I never thought the girls and I would find another chance at family again. Or even want one. But meeting your brother changed everything."

"I'm so glad," Bethany said. Her sister-in-law's joy was so evident.

Elizabeth had been living in Australia with her sister Carly and their parents, performing on the rodeo circuit, when she met Arlo Freeman. Their marriage was a happy one until Arlo sadly died young of cardiac arrest. After feeling lost for two years, Elizabeth had brought her daughters to Montana to meet the rest of the Hawkins family—and when she met Jake McCreery, himself a widower with three children, both families got a fresh start, together.

The waitress came over and took their orders—a BLT for Bethany and a chicken Caesar wrap for Elizabeth. They were splitting a side of sweet potato fries, which Bethany had been craving all day.

"And how are *you* feeling?" Elizabeth asked. "I hope it's okay that Jake shared the big news with me. Pregnant! I'm so excited for you, Bethany."

"Of course it's okay. You're family!" She told Elizabeth the story about Rexx, including finally calling him the other day only to find out he'd changed his number. Then she found herself sharing everything that had happened with Theo.

Elizabeth's eyes widened a few times as Bethany relayed the story, from their conversation at the wedding to her unexpected delivery last night to Theo showing her how to use the mobile's app. "He ordered an entire nursery for you?" she asked as the waitress set down their food.

Bethany swiped a fry in ketchup. "This morning I almost wondered if I dreamed the whole thing. Pregnant women are supposed to have vivid, intense dreams, right? But when I went into the spare bedroom, there it all was. The stack of pj's almost made me burst into tears."

Except for her parents and her brother, who had ever done anything like this for Bethany? No one, she full well knew. Even when she'd had boyfriends over the years, a few that had lasted a year, none had ever doted on her the way Theo had. One guy had broken up with her after she told him she had the flu and asked if he'd drop off chicken soup. *Sorry, but I have a big meeting at work in a couple days and can't afford to catch anything.* Another had insisted she and her band perform at his cousin's destination wedding in Mexico for free and that she and the guys would have to pay for their flights and hotel rooms. He'd dumped her when she said they had a *paying* gig that night.

Yet here was a guy she wasn't even dating who'd spent hours assembling baby equipment he'd also spent hours buying—and researching—for her.

"To make matters worse—or more confusing," Bethany said, "he's ready for marriage. He wants to find his other half."

"Theo Abernathy is probably the most eligible bachelor in Bronco," Elizabeth agreed. "He could have his pick of twenty-two-year-olds who might be looking for rich husbands but aren't necessarily ready for motherhood. That he hasn't been dating a slew of young beauty pageant winners is telling. That he's fallen for you—even *more* telling."

Bethany shook her head. "I don't know about *fallen*. And I'm not so sure he'll change his mind about wanting to be a parent. Maybe in the abstract, he might. But I'm having a baby in a few months. That makes it very real."

"I see him coming around," Elizabeth said, biting into

a fry. "You know that saying, he doesn't know what hit him? Theo doesn't know what's *hitting* him. He's right in the middle of it."

Bethany smiled. "Well, maybe. Oh, wait—then again, maybe not. We're babysitting his year-old nephew tonight, and he'll likely know by the end of the evening if he could see fatherhood for himself."

Elizabeth's eyes widened again, and she pointed another fry at Bethany. "He asked you to *babysit* with him?"

"Don't read too much into that," Bethany said. "I'd just told him how I was a little scared about impending motherhood, that the last time I held a baby was, like, five years ago. So that's why he invited me along tonight. For a little on-the-job training."

"He sure is looking out for you. And wants to spend time with you. In quite a domestic setting," Elizabeth added with a grin. "Mark my words, the man has it bad for you."

Bethany's heart lifted—then deflated a bit. "He's been so up front about his feelings, though. I mean, he told me straight out in our first conversation—which was at your wedding, by the way—that he won't be ready for fatherhood for five years."

"Well, that was then, hon. For a guy who doesn't want to be a dad, he sure is overly focused on a pregnant woman."

Bethany took a bite of her BLT. That was true. He was.

"So just how serious is this for you?" Elizabeth asked. "Are you falling in love?"

Bethany couldn't deny it to herself any longer. "He had me at the back rub. I'm definitely falling in love."

Elizabeth's dark eyes twinkled, and she reached over to take both of Bethany's hands for a squeeze. "I have faith in him. Trust me, if Jake and I managed to get married…"

Bethany knew about the obstacles that had stood in the couple's way. After being widowed, Jake and Elizabeth had been afraid to risk loving again, to risk their children getting attached to a parental figure. But the thought of going on without each other had been unbearable.

She wouldn't dare hope that Theo would feel that way about her.

Elizabeth picked up the final bite of her wrap. "Tonight you have a perfect opportunity to show that man what domestic bliss will look like for the two of you as a couple."

Huh. When put like that… Maybe. Unless cute little Frankie Abernathy was a horror show. Gassy, overtired, missing his parents…who knew what could have that baby screeching his head off for the entire time they'd be in charge of caring for him?

Or perhaps he'd be adorable and cooing and sleep most of the time—and show Theo Abernathy the sweet, easy side of parenthood.

This really could go either way.

When Bethany had arrived at Theo's cabin a half hour ago, he'd known immediately that friendship was out of the question. He was just too attracted to her. He had a few female friends and wasn't overcome with the urge to kiss them, touch them, make love with them.

None of them were pregnant either. And Bethany Mc-Creery, in her pale pink dress that very clearly showed her baby bump, *was*.

His only hope was that babysitting Frankie tonight would go terribly, that the baby would remind him that he was as uninterested in parenthood as he thought he was. That when his nephew would be screaming and crying and all red-faced, neither of them able to calm him down, Theo would see that this would be his future with Bethany and her baby.

And that when Jace and Tamara came to pick up Frankie at 9:00 p.m., he would walk away from both taking care of a baby and his unwanted feelings for Bethany. He'd let her go. She might be alone without the father of the child, but she had a wonderful family and friends who'd stand by her and support her throughout the rest of the pregnancy and after.

And Theo could stop living in a state of confusion. He could go back to thinking only of the ranch and his family and his podcast and, yes, himself.

Holding his nephew as he and Bethany walked Jace and Tamara to the door of his cabin, he wondered why she had to be so beautiful. And sexy. Why she'd had to put her long, silky brown hair in a ponytail that exposed her creamy neck. He was even more attracted to her tonight than he had been at her brother's wedding, which was saying something. Back then, he hadn't known she would be a mother in five months.

"Frankie shouldn't give you any trouble," Tamara said, caressing her son's soft brown hair. "He's such a good baby."

"Unless he gets cranky because he's teething," Jace added with a grin. He dropped a kiss on his son's head.

"Any tips or tricks if he does?" Bethany asked.

"He has a few teething toys he liked chewing on. And he does like being tickled," Jace said, giving the baby's belly a rub.

"Oh, and he loves when you give his ears a little tug. I don't know why, but he does. It makes him hoot with laughter."

"And watch your ponytail," Tamara said to Bethany. "Frankie's a grabber. He loves noses, eyeglasses, ponytails, earrings, and scarves."

"Uh-oh," Bethany said on a chuckle. "I've got two of those, so there's that."

"And if you burp him, make sure you have a burp cloth somewhere in the vicinity of his mouth," Jace added. "Theo learned that lesson last week."

Theo laughed. "I'm still traumatized."

His brother and sister-in-law said their final goodbyes and were gone. They'd left behind their precious baby, his portable playpen, and his car seat. Plus a backpack containing a few necessities, like diapers and wipes. Theo had offered to babysit at their place with the well-stocked nursery, but Jace had said something about wanting Frankie to get used to other environments like his aunts' and uncles' homes.

"Can I hold him?" Bethany asked.

"Sure," he said, transferring Frankie into her arms. Luckily the baby went to her easily, his big eyes alert on her face. In fact, he wouldn't stop staring at her.

Bethany giggled. "He likes me!"

"Who wouldn't like you?" Theo asked, then felt his cheeks warm. He hadn't meant to say that aloud. Something that happened a lot when he was around her. Things just flew out of his mouth, straight from his head, straight from his heart.

"Hear that, Frankie?" Bethany said, her smile so warm he could tell she was touched.

He inwardly frowned. Wasn't this whole night supposed to go south? It was off to *too* good of a start. Frankie was being cute and easy. Bethany was drawing Theo in just by being herself.

Bethany glanced around. "Cabin, huh? My version of a cabin is the kind of place my family went to on summer vacations every other year. A one-room log structure with a loft for me and Jake and barely indoor plumbing. This is…a mansion."

He saw her taking in the luxe-rustic beams and big stone fireplace, the wall of windows with the view of the woods and mountains, the expensive leather sofas and soft rugs. "I think my parents went a little hog wild on the cabins for their children so that they'd keep us on the Bonnie B for all time. But hey, it worked. We all love our homes and living right on the ranch. And it's nice to be so close to one another."

"That *is* nice. Anytime I thought about leaving Bronco and moving someplace that seemed more exciting, I'd picture my family, and I knew I'd never live anywhere else."

He nodded. "Same."

"You'd miss this little guy too much," she said, giving Frankie a little bounce. "And your other nephews and niece."

"Exactly. But after babysitting or getting together, it's also nice to be able to say, 'See ya tomorrow,' and go home to a quiet house and do whatever I want."

"It's funny," she said. "I feel like I've been doing that for thirty-five years. I have a little *too* much free time."

Touché, he thought, considering they were the same age. "I guess there's never really free time when it comes to working on a ranch. Even with my siblings and dad and the employees, there's always work to be done, whether in the office or the range." That was true; despite being management, Theo often got out his toolbox to mend a broken fence or he'd groom a horse or ride out with the herd of cattle, but he also had to admit he'd also do those things when he was feeling particularly restless. When it would hit hard that he really did want a wife to share his life with. And that none of his recent relationships had worked out. And yes, because the past three, all women he liked and respected, kept bringing up wanting to start a family very soon. But it hadn't been just that. Theo had been aware that something bigger, less tangible, was just missing.

Like what he had, what he felt, when he was with Bethany.

"How about you give me and Frankie the grand tour of your 'cabin'?" she asked. "I'd love to see the place."

"We can start right here in the foyer. This is one of my favorite spots in the house, because when I walk in, my eye goes to the grand staircase and the fireplace beyond it. I always give a happy sigh when I walk in the door."

She grinned. "I like my place, but I definitely don't have that same reaction."

"Have you thought about my offer to move into a cabin? Say the word, and I can have your furniture brought over."

The grin faded fast. "Theo, I appreciate that. But I'm fine where I am for the time being. Even if the time being is, like, another month."

He nodded. Five minutes ago he was thinking how he needed to walk away from Bethany. Now he was almost pressuring her to move a quarter mile down the path into a guest cabin?

His feelings were all over the place. He had to get a handle on himself, how he *felt*.

To get his mind off her, he led the way to the kitchen.

"Wow, I hope you cook," she said, looking around the large room. "There's no way you could let the state-of-the-art everything in here go to waste."

"Actually, I'm not much of a cook. I'm fine with the basics—burgers, pasta, chili—but my siblings would disagree." He smiled and turned to her. "I can whip us up dinner when Frankie goes to bed."

"Sounds good. I had an early dinner at the diner with my sister-in-law, but to be honest, I'm craving spaghetti Bolognese. Is that in your repertoire?"

"Spaghetti and meat sauce are staples I always have, so your wish is my command. Tamara told me that we should put Frankie down at seven thirty, so I'll start cooking right after. Apparently, he loves the playpen and falls asleep in a snap. They say he's easy to transfer out too, like out of his car seat and into his crib. A good sleeper."

"God, I hope this little one will be too," she said, tapping her hand on her belly and then putting her arm back around Frankie. "I do love to sleep—especially after a late-night gig. I'm really looking forward to giving myself maternity leave for three months. The guys are going to hold auditions for a temporary replacement, so I'm glad about not leaving them high and dry." She frowned for a second. "I hope she's not so good that they want to permanently replace me."

He reached a hand to her shoulder. "No one could ever compare to you, Bethany."

Her warm smile went straight to his heart. "Aww, thank you. That means a lot."

Okay, he had to get away from that smile. He turned and headed to the living room.

"I spend most of my free time in here," he said. "I love

the view of the woods and mountains. And even in summer, this fireplace makes me happy."

"It's easily the biggest fireplace I've ever seen. I love all the photos on the mantel." She brought Frankie over and peered at them. They were all of the family. "You definitely didn't have an awkward stage," she said, looking at a photo of him as a middle schooler holding a fish he'd just caught.

"Two minutes after my dad snapped that photo of me, my youngest sister, Stacy, caught her first fish, and it was five times the size of mine." He smiled at the picture, remembering that day.

Bethany laughed. "Don't tell Jake I said so, but I always catch a bigger fish than he does."

They moved to the deck, the warm, breezy air refreshing. He hadn't even realized how hot and bothered Bethany had him because of the central air-conditioning. But out here, he was aware of just how heated he was.

Frankie's gaze was on a white butterfly flapping its wings slowly as it landed on a flower lining the patio. The baby pointed, and when the butterfly flew up, Frankie laughed so loud that Theo could hardly believe such a sound could come out of tiny body.

"There is no better sound," she said. "I say that as a singer and a music lover."

"I have to agree. *I* say that as Uncle Theo, always happy to come home to this quiet house. But I could listen to that laughter all day."

Bethany smiled and gave Frankie a nuzzle with her nose on his cheek. "You are such a cutie-pie," she said to the baby.

Frankie immediately grabbed her ponytail—and hung on.

"Oops," Theo said. He stepped close to Bethany, so

close he could smell her shampoo, and tried to gently extricate the baby's fist from her hair. No go.

Bethany smiled. "Well, thanks, but as long as he doesn't start pulling, I'm fine."

Frankie pulled.

"Owie," she said, laughing. "How are you all of what—twenty pounds?—and so strong?"

Theo gave the baby's neck a little tickle, and Frankie laughed and magically let go.

"Success!" Theo said. He held out his arms for the baby, and Bethany handed him over. He kissed Frankie's impossibly soft cheek as Bethany straightened her ponytail.

They went back inside for the rest of the tour. He led her upstairs and showed her his bedroom. He tried not to look at his king-size bed, because he'd immediately imagine Bethany lying naked on his sheets. He hurriedly showed her the two guest rooms.

"Wow, so there are three en suite bathrooms up here," she said, eyeing the marble floor, "and then a full and half bath downstairs. Good Lord."

He nodded. "Told you, my folks spared no expense for comfort. I'll live here forever, and one day my children will and my grandchildren and so on and so on."

She smiled thoughtfully. "That's the first time I've heard you say the words *my children*."

He felt a frown tugging at his mouth and tried to keep his expression neutral. "Well, in the future, I mean. The distant future. Far distant."

She bit her lip and nodded, then quickly turned. "Thanks for the tour. Your house is amazing. How it manages to be so welcoming and cozy, I can't understand."

He wouldn't tell her about the interior designer he'd hired with exactly those directives.

"I have my own set of Frankie's favorite toys in a chest in the living room," he said. "Up for building a very short tower of blocks?"

"Always," she said with a smile.

They sat down on the plush rug, Theo opening the toy chest and taking out the big pouch with the blocks inside. Bethany set Frankie down, and he immediately pulled up on the chest and looked inside.

"Ooh, is he walking yet?" Bethany asked, her arm protectively stretching out behind the baby.

"No," Theo said. "He's pulling up a lot but still hasn't taken his first steps. I sure hope he doesn't tonight while we're babysitting. Jace and Tamara will definitely want to see that big milestone themselves."

"Hear that, Frankie?" Bethany said. "Save your first steps for your parents!"

Frankie moved backward and plopped down to sit. Theo poured out the blocks, and for the next twenty minutes, they watched the baby pick up blocks and set them back down. He hasn't started stacking yet, but according to Jace, that should be coming soon.

After blocks, they watched Frankie crawl around the rug to look at the toys they'd set up. Frankie really loved a certain stuffed monkey and grabbed it, shaking it like crazy. A half hour later, after rounds of peekaboo and a made-up story by Uncle Theo about a calf named Bugz, Frankie started yawning.

"Right on time," Theo said. "Seven thirty and beddy-bye time."

"I guess you'll change him and then put him in the playpen?" Bethany asked.

"Yup. You can have the honors, if you'd like."

Her beautiful face lit up. "I am actually dying to change a diaper. It's been a few years."

He laughed. "Be my guest—*please*." They headed into the bathroom, which had a diaper station for Frankie. He stood in the doorway while she laid Frankie down and gave his tummy a tickle, then made quick work of changing his diaper and zipping his pj's back up.

"All done," she said, scooping up the baby and cuddling him close. "You are so precious," she whispered.

She looked so beautiful, the expression on her face so moving that Theo took his phone from his pocket and quickly snapped a photo. Bethany looked at him in surprise.

No one was more surprised than *he* was.

"I'll send it to you," he said.

"Why'd you take it?" she asked, putting him on the spot. Not purposely, he could see. She was looking at him with genuine curiosity.

"Just the look on your face," he said honestly. "Like Frankie is the eighth wonder of the world."

She laughed. "I kind of feel that way. Babies are remarkable."

He held up the photo on his phone.

"Aww, I see now," she said. She put her hand over her heart.

He quickly texted her the photo, then put his phone away before he got in more trouble.

Back in the living room, Bethany laid Theo down in the playpen. He stretched out, his eyes drifting closed, then opening, then closing again. He let out a little whine and seemed to be fighting sleep, but then he closed his eyes for good, his bow lips quirking up a bit.

"Could it really be that easy?" she asked. "I definitely don't remember that from babysitting my niece and nephews."

"They did say Frankie was easy, and I guess it wasn't a lie to get me to babysit." He chuckled, gently caressing the baby's soft brown hair. "I've watched him a few times over the past year, and he hasn't always been so compliant."

Bethany laughed and looked down at the baby. "Well, Frankie, thank you for the great reintroduction to baby care. Good night."

Theo gave his little nephew one last sweet look. "Now to the kitchen so I can make dinner," he said, leading the way. But he quickly stopped. "Why don't you sit and relax in the living room. Are you tired?" he asked, peering at her. "I read on a pregnancy website that women get more fatigued as the months progress."

Bethany stopped in her tracks. "Pregnancy website? Were you doing some research?"

He bit his lip. "Just a little. To see what you'd be going through."

Bethany burst into tears. She covered her face with her hands.

Okay, this was unexpected. "What did I say? Bethany?"

She dropped her hands and wiped under her eyes. "You're everything I want, Theo Abernathy. A man who's reading up on month four of pregnancy? Rare. Trust me. It's just all too much. Everything."

Ah. Now he felt like a bigger heel than he had all along. Especially because they'd both shaken on friendship again. The big problem was that he couldn't be her friend. And he'd been unwittingly making her feel like he was the man of her dreams.

"Theo, I like you—a lot." She bit her lip, her beautiful eyes full of…disappointment. Sadness. *Oh, Bethany.* "And to protect myself, like I said yesterday I had to do, I'm gonna go. I can't do this. How can we be friends when there's so much more between us? That's not going to work."

He sucked in a breath. He wished he could say the right thing. But what was that? What could he say? He felt how he felt.

"I understand, Bethany. I wish I could just make you dinner first, though. I make a really good Bolognese sauce."

"You're making things worse, not better, Theo." She gave him a shaky smile. "I'm gonna go."

He should be grateful that she was making this so much easier for him. She was the one ending their friendship. She was letting him off the hook.

But the sharp ache in his chest told him that, once again, he didn't understand why he was feeling so torn up about it.

You're not willing to really think about how much you feel for Bethany.

She walked over to the playpen and bent down. "Good night, sweet Frankie." Then she straightened and headed for the door.

He followed, his stomach twisting when she opened the door. *Don't let her walk out of your life.*

He had to. For both their sakes.

He walked her to her car, and she got in without a word. She did look at him briefly before turning to reverse.

And then she was gone.

Chapter Thirteen

His heart heavy, Theo went back inside and paced in front of the wall of windows. What the hell he was supposed to do?

He paced and sat, paced and sat. He spent a good twenty minutes just watching his nephew sleep, the little chest rising and falling.

"I'm sorry, Frankie, but I'm not ready for you—my *own* you. That's just the truth."

With that clear in his head, he wheeled the playpen into his home office, which he'd turned into his podcast recording studio. He got everything set up to record the start of a new episode, an intro about the rancher he'd be interviewing in a few days.

As he hit Record and started speaking, he realized about twenty minutes later that he'd recorded the entire introduction and Frankie never made a peep.

"Well, my *own* baby won't be easy like you are," Theo said as he wheeled the playpen back into the living room and then set the diaper bag next to it. Jace and Tamara would be stopping by any minute to pick up their son. "And Bethany's baby will be a really difficult baby, probably," he said. "Murphy's law, right?" He tried to smile since it was just a joke, but he couldn't.

And suddenly, Theo himself could burst into tears. Something was just very wrong with him right now. His emotions were all over the place. He didn't even know this Theo Abernathy. It was as though *he* was the hormonal one.

His phone pinged with a text, which he hoped was from Bethany, but it was Jace. They were here and didn't want to ring the doorbell just in case it woke Frankie.

He opened the door as Tamara and Jace came up the steps.

"Was Frankie a good little guy for you and Bethany?" Tamara asked.

"Frankie was great. I, on the other hand…" Theo said with a frown.

"What's wrong?" Tamara asked, peering behind him and realizing that Bethany wasn't there.

"It's a long story," he said as they came inside. "No, it's a short story."

"What, Theo?" Tamara asked, looking at him with concern.

He sighed and dropped down on the edge of the sofa. "Bethany's pregnant and I'm crazy about her. But I'm not ready to be a dad. It's not what I want right now. So I need to let her go. Not that it's my choice—I upset her and she left."

"But you saw how easy taking care of Frankie is," Jace said. "To be very honest, it's why I asked you to babysit."

Theo narrowed his eyes at his brother. "I thought you asked because no one else was available."

Jace had the decency to look sheepish. "Okay, fine, Robin and Stacy were both free tonight. And Mom and Dad. But after our last conversation about Bethany, I wanted you to see what a total joy a baby is. And that they sleep a lot."

"I did get to see that," Theo admitted. "I even got the intro of this week's podcast done. Frankie napped like a champ. But I don't kid myself that that's what parenthood is like."

"You shouldn't," Tamara said. "Parenthood is no cakewalk. It's the most rewarding thing I've ever experienced, but it's also hard. You're right to take your time in figuring out how you feel."

Theo nodded. "Except Bethany left because we can't even be *friends*."

"Bro," Jace said. "Fix that."

"How? How can I be friends with a woman I'd marry in a heartbeat if she wasn't pregnant?"

Tamara stared at him. "God, Theo. Did you hear what you just said?"

"What?" he asked, looking from Jace to Tamara, who were staring at each other in a kind of disbelief.

"Theo, honey, think about it," Tamara said gently. "That's your job for tonight. Think long and hard about what you just said."

Theo dropped his head back and ran a hand through his hair. "I *can't* think. It's why I'm at this stalemate with myself."

"So you're gonna give up the woman you *would* marry because she's pregnant?" Jace asked. "Dude."

"If he doesn't want to be a father yet," Tamara said, "then he's doing the right thing."

I am, right? Theo wondered. *How could the right thing feel so wrong, though?*

But what else could he do? He wasn't ready for his entire life to change so drastically in five months.

"Maybe I'm just too set in my ways," Theo said.

Jace nodded. "Nothing wrong with knowing who you are and what you want. That's why you're pushing back against the idea of fatherhood. Because of how responsible you'd be if you had a child."

Exactly what he'd thought in Hey, Baby when he'd encountered the bickering parents.

But it just left him more confused than ever.

"Sometimes," Jace added, "when I'm really busy and Frankie is sick or cranky, and Tamara and I can't get a sitter, I envy your carefree life. But honestly, I don't right now. This is tough stuff."

Yeah, Theo thought, his heart aching. It was.

Chapter Fourteen

At eight thirty the next morning, Bethany sat at the kitchen table of her mother's house, drinking decaf and trying to concentrate on her mother's lists. Raye McCreery had four going, all on paper in her notebook—the old-fashioned way.

Thank heavens they'd had these early-morning plans. Because Bethany had woken up all puffy eyed from crying and needing a comforting place to go. And that was always her mother. It was hard to leave Theo's last night and go home to all those reminders of him in her spare bedroom. In the *nursery*. She'd tossed and turned and kept waking up.

"Okay," her mom said, tapping her pen against the page, "I have the necessity list, the wish list, the get-it-before-the-baby-comes list and the get-it-after list." She took a sip of her coffee. "Let's start with necessities. I can cross off or add, so this is just off the top of my head and from consulting lists online."

Bethany instantly thought of Theo googling away on his phone to find out what was happening in month four of pregnancy. *Don't think about him*, she ordered herself.

But how could she not? Especially when she and her mom were talking about things she needed for the baby.

"Okay," her mom said, taking a sip of her coffee, then

grabbing her pen and reading from the list labeled *Necessities*. "Infant car seat. Stroller. Crib. Maybe a bassinet too that can be easily moved. A playpen—portable. Changing table and pad. Maybe a dresser combo, even though you have a dresser in the spare bedroom. Infant bathtub, baby wash, thermometer, infant OTC medications, pj's, onesies, socks, booties, diapers, ointments, and cornstarch." She tapped her pen at the end of the list. "My goodness— those are just the necessities! And I might be forgetting a few things."

Bethany started mentally adding up the costs of some of that—what she didn't already have. Goodness, people weren't kidding when they said children were expensive. "Well, you can cross a few things off the list," Bethany said. "In my spare bedroom—in the nursery, I should say— is now a beautiful bassinet with an adorable mobile that plays lullabies and spins little dangling stuffed animals, a top-of-the-line baby bouncer, a changing table, ten newborn-sized pj's and a pair of baby booties." Plus the pair of yellow pj's and a stuffed rabbit she'd bought the day she'd found out she was pregnant.

"You bought all that?" Raye asked, surprise on her face.

"Actually, they were gifts," Bethany said. "From Theo Abernathy."

Her mother tilted her head. "Theo Abernathy—one of Bonnie and Asa's sons, right?"

She nodded. Everyone knew the Abernathys in Bronco, whether you lived in the Heights or the Valley. They were a prominent, altruistic family and their names came up often, particularly around the holidays, since they did a lot of sponsoring.

"There has to be a story here," her mom said. Waiting.

Bethany inwardly sighed. Talking about it would just get her all upset again. But she needed to get it all out— and hear her mother's thoughts.

"Let me catch you up," Bethany said, and it all came pouring out. Starting with Theo at the wedding, then the latest about Rexx, then more about Theo, ending with what happened last night.

"Oh, Bethany," her mother said, touching her arm. "That's a *lot*."

She nodded. "And now it's over. Before it even began. Wait, scratch that. It did begin."

"Yeah, I'd say quite a bit happened in your relationship. Do you really think he's just going to walk away? I can't see how."

Bethany wouldn't have thought so either. But last night, he'd sounded so resolute. Just as he always had.

"He knows how he feels about being a parent right now," Bethany said. "That's never changed. He just happened to fall in like with a woman who's pregnant."

Her mother sipped her coffee. "Sounds more like love to me."

I wish. If he did love her, he'd never be able to let her go. So of course he didn't love her.

"He's just a nice guy," Bethany said, feeling tears poke at her eyes.

"There's a difference between nice and inviting you on a walk around his family ranch. Ordering a bassinet and mobile and assembling both. Buying ten pairs of pj's in the correct size. Making you pizza. Inviting you to baby-sit with him. Offering to make you spaghetti Bolognese."

"Don't forget the baby booties," Bethany said—and then she did cry.

"Oh, honey." Her mom got up and stood behind Bethany's chair and wrapped her arms around her. "The man is going through big changes. He met you and didn't expect to have his feelings challenged."

Huh. She hadn't really thought about it that way.

"I have a good feeling about the two of you, honey," her mom added.

Bethany brightened a bit at that. "Elizabeth said she did too. But I'm afraid to hope. I thought leaving his house before he had a chance to make me that romantic-sounding dinner meant I was going to save myself from a world of hurt. But I'm hurting, anyway."

In fact, she was *physically* hurting. Her belly—low in her belly—was suddenly cramping. She put her hand where the sharp pain was coming from. "Ow," she said, frowning.

"Bethany?" her mom asked. "What's wrong?"

"Ow," she said again, doubling over.

"I'm taking you to the emergency clinic right now," her mom said, sounding panicked. "Can you stand?"

Bethany tried to move and winced.

"I'm going to call your OB. Honey, hang on, okay? I'll be right back." Her mother ran from the room to get her phone.

Bethany let out a bunch of short breaths, hoping it would ease the pain. But the sharp, stabbing sensations kept coming.

What was this? Something to worry about? Something serious? Or normal aches and pains? She couldn't remember reading about a stabbing pain in the lower belly.

Scared out of her mind, Bethany felt a little better when her mother rushed back into the kitchen, on the phone with the OB. "Dr. Rangely wants you to go the hospital right away. She's at the clinic, but she'll meet us there."

Bethany let her mother ease her up from the chair. *Please let everything be okay*, she prayed.

Suddenly, all she wanted besides good news about the pains was Theo by her side.

After a rough night of thinking about Bethany and all that had happened, how they'd left things last night, Theo finally got out of bed and took a hot shower.

He stared at himself in the mirror—he looked like hell, like a man who hadn't slept. Like a man who'd lost something precious to him.

He threw his towel at the mirror and got dressed, then sucked down a cup of coffee. He had to do something to fix things between him and Bethany—something to clear the air.

And then what? He didn't feel differently. He couldn't change anything. He just hated the way she'd left. The way he'd let her just leave.

He grabbed his car keys and headed out. He had a vague idea that he'd pick up something for Bethany in town— what, he didn't know. As he was about to pass Kendra's Cupcakes, he decided an array of cupcakes would be a nice gesture.

A gesture. Small. Impersonal. Nothing confusing about a box of cupcakes. It would just let her know he was sorry.

It wasn't good enough. But it was something.

He'd drop off the cupcakes at her apartment, she'd say thank you, and then he would leave and at least there wouldn't be the same awful energy between them.

Once he'd given his order to Kendra, he turned to find

none other than Winona Cobbs in line behind him in her trademark purple outfit. He heard laughter and glanced over to see her fiancé, Stanley Sanchez, at the far end of the bakery, chatting with a group.

He looked back to Winona. She was staring at Theo. No expression at all. Just staring. Could she *know* what had happened between him and Bethany last night?

"Morning, Winona," he said, tipping his hat. "I was, uh, thinking of calling you to schedule an appointment." He leaned a bit closer and whispered, "I could use a little wisdom."

He was really doing it. Making an appointment with a psychic. That was how unsettled he was.

"I'll save you the trip," she said, lifting her chin. "What's meant to happen *will*," she added, then practically pushed past him to get to the counter.

He turned to stare at her back, hoping for a little elaboration once she'd ordered.

Her coffee drink in hand, she turned and eyed him. "Like I said, you think you know what you want. But you don't." With that, she simply walked away. He watched her approach Stanley's table, the gentleman pulling out a chair for her.

What he *wanted* was Bethany *and* his life to go on exactly as it always had. That was not going to change. It was also not going to happen.

He sighed and stopped at a chair by the door to call Bethany to make sure she was home; he couldn't exactly leave a box of cupcakes in her unairconditioned tiny lobby on a hot July day. He planned to say that he felt bad about how they'd left things last night and wanted to drop off some treats. He had no idea if she'd hit End Call or if she'd say okay. He never found out because the call went straight to voice mail.

Maybe she was at rehearsal with her band? No—because a black-haired guy in a leather vest at a table in the corner was easily recognizable from the band photo on Bethany's mantel.

Could be that she just wasn't answering, that she was avoiding him, planning to cut him out, ghost him, that she was done.

Not that he could blame her. But now that he was faced with the actual end of their relationship, he couldn't stand it. He cared too much about Bethany McCreery to never talk to her again. To not know how she was doing, feeling, if she needed anything, whether to satisfy a craving or for her baby.

He'd text her. If she didn't respond, he'd have to respect that she didn't want to hear from him.

He typed a simple sentence: Can I stop by for a few minutes?

And waited.

No response.

His heart clenched. For a minute, he could barely breathe.

He had to get through his thick skull that she was done with him.

Theo closed his eyes for a second and got ahold of himself, then headed out, determined to drop off the stupid cupcakes in the ranch office, then hit the range like he always did when he needed to clear his head.

He'd just gotten into his car when his phone pinged with a text. Bethany.

At the clinic's ER. Having bad pains. I'm so scared.

Theo's heart started racing. Bad pains? What could that mean?

On my way, he texted back, then dropped his phone and started the car.

She had to be okay. The baby had to be okay.

He was definitely *not* okay.

Bethany sat on the cot in the recovery room, staring at the curtain pulled around her for privacy. Her OB and the ER doctor had assured her everything was fine—with her and the baby—but they both wanted her to rest in their care for a good half hour before she was discharged. Her mother had gone out to the backyard where there were some tables and chairs to call her father and brother with an update. Just normal bad cramping that might happen occasionally, but Bethany had done the right thing by calling her OB and coming in to be checked out.

Now that she knew the baby was okay, she wished she hadn't texted Theo. What had she been thinking? She knew, actually. Despite what had happened between them last night, when she'd been scared and worried, she'd immediately thought of *him*, wanted *him* by her side.

That was how much he'd come to mean to her. How much she trusted him. Despite everything.

And within seconds, he'd texted back that he was on his way. She'd thought about texting him again that it was a false alarm, no need to come, but she didn't want to do that while she knew he was driving.

She heard his voice from down the hall; he was asking the nurse at the reception desk where to find her. Next she heard footsteps coming her way. Then his voice. "Bethany?"

"Come on in," she called.

He was holding a large box from Kendra's Cupcakes. She hadn't been craving cupcakes, but now she suddenly had to have one.

"Are you okay?" he asked in a rush. "Is the baby okay? What did the doctor say?" His green eyes held so much concern.

She told him what both the ER doc and her OB had said, and she could visibly see him relax, his shoulders unbunching, the color coming back in his face.

That he cared about her had never been in question.

He put the cupcakes on the bedside table and sat in the chair at her side, then held out his arms and she leaned into them, let him hold her.

Tears streamed down her cheeks, and she knew she was crying from the scare and because of how good it felt to be in the warm comfort of Theo Abernathy's arms.

"I'm so relieved," he said, stroking her hair. "I was so scared, Bethany."

"Me too. That was the first time I'd been hit with pains like that. I was at my mom's house when my belly started hurting out of the blue."

"I'm so glad you weren't alone," he said.

Alone. She'd gotten lucky that she'd been at her mom's. But what if the pains happened again and she was alone? She'd be nervous all over again, and Theo would be the one she'd want beside her.

This was crazy. They weren't even friends anymore.

"I'm sorry about the way I ran out last night," she said. "Self-preservation, particularly when pregnant, must be a thing."

She mentally shook her head. She definitely hadn't meant to say that.

"I totally understand, Bethany. I wish I—" He paused and but didn't have to finish the sentence. She knew.

This was a lost cause. She had to let him go. He wasn't going to magically change just because she was in love.

Oh, God. She closed her eyes at the monumental truth. She was in love with Theo Abernathy.

Now she knew why it felt so good *and* hurt so bad to be in his arms.

He held her for a few more seconds, then pulled back when footsteps could be heard coming their way. "Bethany, you decent?"

Her brother.

She gave Theo's hand a squeeze, and he stood up and moved to the side of the small room. "If you consider my flowered hospital gown decent, sure."

Jake, along with their parents and Elizabeth, came in, a flurry of questions and hugs and kisses. They all seemed to freeze with surprise when they noticed Theo, then gathered themselves to nod or say hello.

"Well, I'll leave you to your family," Theo said. "There are enough cupcakes to go around," he added, pointing at the big box.

For the millionth time since her brother's wedding, all she could think was *Oh, Theo*.

Chapter Fifteen

"For God's sake, Theo, just go see her," Billy said.

"Put us all out of our misery," Jace added. "Yourself included."

Theo glanced up at his brothers at their desks in the ranch office, the conversation registering but barely. It was almost 4:00 p.m. and he'd been distracted by thoughts of Bethany all day. He'd shaken salt in his coffee when he'd arrived this morning, despite the fact that the saltshaker required twisting. He'd walked into the wall instead of through the bathroom door. And he'd been unable to make sense of anything he was looking at on his desktop monitor.

Billy took a sip of his coffee. "You've been staring at the same spreadsheet of figures for the past twenty minutes, Theo. Just go talk to Bethany, tell her you love her and are looking forward to fatherhood, and then everyone will be happy."

"I second that motion," Jace said.

From the moment Theo had arrived in the office—after leaving the clinic, he'd taken a ride out on the range to stare at the cattle and mountains—his brothers had been full of advice. None he could take. Jace had told Billy everything that had happened last night—right in front of Theo, so he knew every word was correct.

"You want to marry this woman but you're now not even friends?" Billy asked.

Theo sighed. "It's a moot point. You can stop bringing it up. I only used that word last night to drive home how hard this all is. Yeah, I could see myself getting very serious with Bethany if she wasn't pregnant. Other than that, she's everything I've been looking for. All the feelings I've been looking for."

His brothers were staring at him like he'd grown an extra head.

"Theo," Billy started to say in his I'm-the-older-brother voice.

He held up a hand. "Billy, we—Jace and Tamara and I—talked it out last night. If I'm not ready, I'm not ready. So why should I go see Bethany now? She's fine, just had a scare, and we can both move on with our lives now."

Jace laughed. "I don't recall us reaching any kind of conclusion last night. What I do know is that this morning, the woman informed you that she was having pains and you rushed to the clinic. Neither of you has moved on, Theo."

Theo sighed hard. He took a long slug of his coffee, which still had the faint taste of salt. "I ran into Winona Cobbs at Kendra's Cupcakes this morning. She told me, 'What's meant to happen will.' At first I didn't really get it—it sounded like what I'd pull out of a fortune cookie. But I've been thinking about it all morning, and now I understand the message. What's meant to happen is absolutely nothing."

Jace shook his head. "You're kidding, right? You're on a speeding train to fatherhood, bro. Go get some cigars now."

Billy laughed. "Sorry, Theo, but I agree. I happen to have a few cigars leftover from when Charlotte first told me she was pregnant."

Theo scowled, and his brothers cracked up even harder. Great. Like he needed this?

"In all seriousness, Theo," Jace said, "you should go check in on Bethany. Code of the West pretty much insists on it."

He narrowed his eyes at Jace. "I was thinking I should, anyway. I mean, I do care about the woman."

Billy nodded. "Go now. You'll have to stop to pick up something since you gave the cupcakes to her family." He and Jace shared a grin that Theo caught. "Whatever Bethany is having cravings for."

"Give me some good suggestions," Theo said.

"Charlotte's been craving sour cream and onion potato chips," Billy said. "But my ex only wanted sharp cheddar cheese with a certain kind of crumbly crackers I had to drive forty-five minutes to get."

Billy had gone through a rough divorce, but because he was so in love with fiancée Charlotte Taylor, he could talk about his marriage without the haunted look in his eyes. Now that they were expecting a baby, they liked the idea of getting married before the little one arrived and they were in the throes of wedding planning. Billy had even asked if Theo would check with Bethany about her band performing at the reception. He had no doubt Bethany would be touched about that.

And Theo had to admit that seeing his older brother so happy made Theo feel like anything was possible.

Except when it came to him and fatherhood.

MELISSA SENATE   175

But at the very least, he and Bethany McCreery *were* friends—no matter what either of them said.

"Fine," Theo said. "I'll stop by the diner and bring her an early dinner."

His brothers were chuckling as he left. But as Theo stood to the side of the porch to straighten his Stetson, he also heard Jace say, "The poor guy doesn't know what he's in for."

And Billy respond, "I think he actually does."

Theo scowled again. More doublespeak like Winona! The only thing that was going to happen was that he and Bethany would have to figure out how to be friends. They cared about each other too much to walk away.

He'd go pick up food for Bethany, then stop by for a half hour and bring up the idea of giving friendship another try. What else could they do, right?

He went to the Gemstone Diner, since he knew she liked the place, and texted her.

I'm at the diner and thought I'd stop by with dinner. Craving anything?

Perfect. Sounded like he just happened to be there. And happened to think of her.

Three dots appeared and then disappeared, then reappeared.

Okay, I finally narrowed it down. I'd love a Western omelet with home fries and an English muffin with strawberry jam. And thanks!

Actually, that sounded good to him too. But butter instead of jam.

With cheddar cheese, she added with a smiley face wearing a cowboy hat.

Coming right up, he texted back.

Fifteen minutes later, their orders in hand, he got back in his car and drove to her apartment. She buzzed him in, and when he neared the top step, he could see her standing in the doorway looking so beautiful.

He held up the bag. "I got the same thing as you."

Bethany smiled. "I'm dying for those home fries."

She stopped in the kitchen to grab two bottles of water, and then they sat at the little round table by the window, Theo taking out containers and packets of the strawberry jam for her.

"Did you get cheddar too?" she asked, eyeing the bite of omelet midway to this mouth.

"Actually, it's Swiss."

"Oooh, I'll trade you a bite," she said, her eyes lit up.

Theo laughed. "Deal."

They sure seemed like friends. This was going great.

"I guess we are friends, whether we like it or not," she said as though reading his mind. "And *good* friends, at that."

He smiled and nodded. "We just have to go with it, I guess." *What's meant to happen will*, he thought suddenly, Winona Cobbs's words echoing in his head.

Maybe he'd been wrong about what he thought she'd meant. That *nothing* would happen. Now he was pretty sure Winona had meant that he and Bethany were meant to be friends.

With just crumbs on their plates, Bethany let out a big yawn. He got up and cleaned up the table.

"Thanks, Theo," she said, moving over to the sofa and stretching out. "How about a movie. Thriller?"

"Sounds great," he said. Friendly. And it was early too. He'd be home by eight and would work on his interview questions for the podcast episode.

Yes, this friendship thing was working out fine.

He took the bag and empty containers into the kitchen, and by the time he was back with a bowl of popcorn and more water, Bethany was out cold. He smiled as he watched her sleep, her long, silky hair falling across her face. He moved the strands behind her ear.

Before he could think too much about it, he scooped her up, her arms slinging around his neck with a little sigh that almost undid him. He felt it right in the strain behind his zipper.

"My hero," she murmured as though she were half-asleep, half-awake.

I'm no one's hero, he wanted to say. But for the moment, he liked the sentiment.

He laid her down on her bed, glad she was wearing a T-shirt and yoga pants, which were pajama-like. He slid the blanket folded on the edge of her bed up and over her, and she snuggled in and turned with another sigh, her eyes closed.

He couldn't imagine leaving. As a precaution, he figured he'd stay the night on the couch, just in case she woke up at some point and was disoriented. Or had another scare.

Or just needed...a friend.

Bethany woke to the remnants of another of those vivid, intense pregnancy dreams. Theo had carried her to her bed from the sofa, kissing her all the way there, then laid her down on top of her quilt and peeled off her yoga pants, then her T-shirt. His hands and mouth had roamed everywhere, and finally he'd taken off her bra, feasting on her breasts, then inched down her underwear. He'd started taking off his own T-shirt, revealing rock-hard abs and a faint line of dark hair disappearing into the waistband of his jeans. Oh, how she'd wanted those off. But just as he'd been about to flick the button of his jeans, her eyes had opened.

She was alone in her bedroom. Fully dressed. A strand of hair across her cheek.

Theo was not in bed with her.

Eyes opened wide, she sat up, not sure what time it was. What day it was.

And she remembered—one-sixteenth of her dream had actually been real. Theo had picked her up off the sofa, where she'd been dozing after dinner, and carried her to her bedroom. Not a single kiss. But he had laid her down on her bed.

And left the room.

Was he still here? Probably not. She eyed the alarm clock on the bedside table—1:22 a.m.

She got out of bed and walked lightly to the door, which was ajar, and then pushed it open with a finger, peering into the living room. The lights were all out. The table where they'd had dinner was clear and smelled faintly of the citrus wood cleaner she kept under the sink.

She smiled at how thoughtful the man was. As she stepped farther into the living room, she gasped—Theo Abernathy was stretched out on the sofa, her chenille throw half covering his legs and torso. The moonlight coming from the window softly illuminated him, his thick, tousled dark hair, the fringe of dark eyelashes against his cheeks. The way his shoulders filled out that Henley T-shirt.

Part of her, a big part, wanted to take off her clothes and wake him up with a kiss. Or more. In the dream, he'd been about to unbutton his jeans. She could simply finish that for him.

If she were more brazen.

If they were on the same page.

She tiptoed over to him and pulled the throw up a bit since the windows were open to bring in the summer night breeze. His eyes opened.

"Mmm," he whispered—as if he'd been having a hot dream of his own.

"Sorry I woke you," she said. "I just wanted to pull the blanket up a little."

He sat up, running a hand through his hair. "I didn't want to just leave while you were asleep. I thought I'd sit on the sofa till you woke up, but you never did and I guess I fell asleep too."

"You're a sweet guy, Theo," she said, unable to take her eyes off him as her dream replayed in her head. "I had a really sexy dream about you," she dared to add.

"Oh, yeah?" he asked, his voice a bit ragged.

She nodded. "You carried me to my bed, but instead of leaving the room, you undressed me. Touched me, kissed me everywhere. You were about to take off your jeans when I woke up."

She saw him swallow.

She wanted the dream to become reality. All of it.

Every inch of her body was tingling. With desire. Need.

Go for it, she told herself. *Put yourself out there. You want this man. Even if it's just for tonight, you'll always have the memories.*

"I think we can make that dream come true," she said before she chickened out.

He was looking at her, intently, desire in the green depths of his eyes. His expression was serious, as though he was restraining himself, controlling the urge to pull her onto him.

"And I'm not talking about friends with benefits," she said. "That never works. I'm talking about just tonight. One night only."

"Are you sure?" he whispered.

"One hundred percent."

He studied her for a moment, and she knew he was giving her time to back out and making a decision himself.

He took her hands and gently tugged her toward him so that there was nowhere to go but on him, to straddle him. Her softness met his hardness, and she wrapped her arms around his neck, pressing into him. He groaned and kissed her. A long, hot, passionate kiss.

Then he picked her up and carried her toward the bedroom. "Tell me everything I did in the dream," he said.

She smiled as her nerve endings lit up. "You kissed me the entire way to my bed."

He bent to kiss her, his tongue trailing along her lips, then down to her neck and collarbone. She moaned and scratched at his back. If he could get her this hot and bothered by kissing her…

He used his foot to push open her bedroom door, then resumed kissing her all the way to the bed.

As he laid her down and then covered her body with his own, but propped up on his strong forearms, he said, "It's safe?"

"Absolutely," she assured him. "Doc said so."

His hand was cupping her cheek, and he was looking at her suddenly with more tenderness than desire.

Noooo. Please do not get up. Please do not say this is a bad idea. For tonight, it's a great idea.

"I've wanted to rip your clothes off from the moment I saw you on stage at your brother's wedding," he said. "And every day since."

"Same here."

He was looking at her again, giving her time to tell him they couldn't do this, shouldn't do this. That it would only make her want him more. And who knew how it would affect him?

She bit her lip. She should put a stop to this.

But she looked at his face, his gorgeous face, and the muscles of his arms, his long, strong body, and she wanted him so badly that the fallout would be worth it. No matter what the future brought, they would have tonight.

"To tonight," she said. "I'm raising a pretend drink. A Shirley Temple."

He smiled. "To tonight."

And then her dream started to come true, bit by bit. Her T-shirt was peeled off, and she heard his sharp intake of breath as he gazed at her breasts barely contained by the bra that had recently become too small. A moment of insecurity hit her. Would the baby bump send him running?

It didn't. His hands didn't sweep over it, but then again, at the moment, they were headed north, caressing her breasts, his mouth following. She wasn't sure if he was purposely trying to be tender, but everything he did was just right.

The bra had a front closure, and she undid it, the serious anticipation on his face making her toes curl. His hands and mouth and tongue explored every bit of her bare breasts and her nipples, one moment tenderly, the next passionately, and both felt so damned good.

She reached to get his shirt off, and he lifted his arms. His chest, his shoulders, his stomach—all things of muscled beauty. His body was rock hard, rancher hard. He carefully flipped them so that she was on top of him. She dragged her lips down his neck, across his collarbone to his pecs. Then she kissed a trail lower to his stomach. Finally, they were up to the part of the dream where his jeans would be unbuttoned. She took care of that, his eyes never leaving her face, and as she pulled down the zipper he groaned and sat up, getting the jeans off and making quick work of taking off her yoga pants.

Now they were both in their underwear. His gaze traveled her body, and he groaned, his hands back on her breasts, one going into her hair as he lay back down. She moved against him and he groaned again, then reached to peel off her underwear. She shimmied it off.

Bethany straddled him, using her teeth to pull down his sexy black boxer briefs.

As he got them the rest the way off, she wrapped a hand around his impressive erection, tightly, and he arched his back and almost grunted, delighting her. She moved her hand up and down, lying on top of him and kissing his chest and neck.

His mouth fused to hers, he flipped her over again. She could feel him reaching down to the floor as if looking for something. He had his jeans in his hands, then his wallet, then a foil-wrapped condom. Theo Abernathy, always prepared.

She did the honors, his groans and eyes closing in concentration to control himself making her feel like the sexiest woman alive.

And then he was inside her, thrusting gently at first, again obviously trying to keep in control, and then so passionately she screamed and dug her nails into his shoulders.

Waves of sensation released in such pleasure that she screamed his name and felt him thrusting hard, exploding at the same time. She pulled him into her embrace, spent and sated.

One night of that—this—would never be enough. How could she ever get enough of this man? Or let him go?

"That was amazing," he whispered, stroking her hair. "*You're* amazing."

"Takes two to tango," she said with a grin and kissed his cheek. It might be last time she got to do that. She'd take every moment of tonight. It had to last for the rest of her life. Because she couldn't imagine ever feeling this way about another man.

A lump formed in her throat, and she blinked back threatening tears.

She loved him. She loved Theo Abernathy.

"Bethany, in all honesty, there's no way this can be a onetime thing for me."

She could have cried. She squeezed her eyes shut, so moved, so hopeful, and then propped up on an elbow. "What are you saying?"

"I'm saying I can't get enough of you. That's all I know."

She inwardly gasped. The very thought she'd had about him. Her heart soared. She could almost hear her friends whispering in her ear to be careful. As much as they were all for this romance and its possibilities, her besties had cautioned her to believe what he *said* even if his actions said something else—like that he loved her. "It's the same for me, Theo. Maybe we should just take this one day a time. No labels. No talking about the future."

He nodded. "Deal." He kissed her on the lips, nestled beside her and wrapped his arms around her. She rested her head on his chest, so in love she thought she might burst.

She had no idea what would happen in five months. Heck, she had no idea what would happen next week or even tomorrow.

But they were together right now, naked and breathing hard, neither willing to walk away from this beautiful encounter they'd had.

And she was going with it.

Chapter Sixteen

With each passing day since Theo had first slept with Bethany, he was more and more of a wreck. He couldn't sleep. He couldn't concentrate.

And despite his worries about dating a pregnant woman, he couldn't get enough of Bethany.

Just like he'd told her the night they'd slept together and had kept telling her in the three days that had passed since. He'd stayed over that night, so enthralled by her and how good they were in bed that he hadn't thought beyond the morning, when he'd gotten up early to make her breakfast. They'd spent the next two nights in his house, and when his brothers had seen him walking her out to her car in the mornings, they'd grinned and wolf whistled. In the office, he'd told him that he and Bethany were taking it day by day.

There'd been no talk about the future.

Jace had said he thought that was asking for trouble, because the future was right in front of his face in the form of Bethany's belly.

Billy had added that Theo might as well just accept now that his life was about to change with hers.

And Theo would smile and nod—while his stomach churned, his shoulders bunched, and his brain short-circuited. He'd never felt less like himself than the past few days.

That couldn't be good. Or right.

But he was trying. Trying to give this a chance, to be with Bethany, to think about exactly what this relationship would mean for him. The first morning he'd woken up with her, he'd thought that maybe he could do this. That maybe he had to stop being so stubborn, so selfish, if that was the right word. Was he being selfish by not wanting his great life to change so drastically—yet? He still wasn't sure about that.

But he was sure he wasn't ready.

This he kept from Bethany. He didn't want to play out his confusion with her. They'd agreed not to talk about the future—which was coming in under five months and then every day after that till forever. Maybe he had to give himself more time. To open himself up to change. To his life being turned upside down.

True to her word, she didn't bring up November, when she was due. She talked about the pregnancy but not about the delivery. And thereafter. Sometimes, he'd catch her deep in thought and knew she was worried, but he'd just take her hand or hold her in a sort of silent acknowledgment.

Maybe Jace was right—that he and Bethany were existing in a bubble where there was no baby to deal with. To take care of. And the rude awakening was coming fast.

Theo sighed hard and left the ranch office and walked the half mile to his cabin. In those fifteen minutes, he'd gone back and forth about it all. *Yes, I can do this. No, I can't.*

All he knew was that Bethany was worth all the soul-searching. He didn't have answers to the father question, but he knew *that*.

He pulled out his phone to check the time. In fifteen

minutes, a new rancher was coming to be interviewed for Theo's *This Ranching Life* podcast. Theo admired the guy. Paul was in his early twenties, a new father to a three-month-old daughter, and had taken over his late grandfather's small, failing cattle ranch, determined to keep the family legacy going, to make his grandfather proud.

Theo was glad he'd made it a habit to arrange for the fees for the commercial spots to be paid into a fund to benefit ranchers in need. Like this young family. He hadn't missed the catch in the guy's voice when Theo had told him that he'd be turning over the revenue from the podcast episode to him. It was a good amount of money that would turn a corner for the ranch. Plus, *This Ranching Life* was popular in town and the county, and the new rancher would find himself getting emails and calls for freebies. Bronco was that kind of place.

Theo headed into his home office, where he'd just gotten the equipment set up when he heard a truck pulling up outside and went out to welcome his guest.

Theo couldn't have been more surprised to see Paul, a lanky blond in head-to-toe denim except for his brown leather cowboy boots, walking toward the porch holding a pink car seat—with a baby in it.

"Theo, I'm real sorry about this," Paul said, "but my wife is feeling really ill and I couldn't find a sitter. Maya here is a champion napper and she should fall asleep for a good hour and a half in about five minutes."

"Perfect," Theo said. "Beautiful baby," he added, bending a bit to play a round of peekaboo with Maya. Frankie loved peekaboo.

"Waaaah!" the baby girl screeched. Her face turned red.

"Sorry," Theo said to Paul. "Babies usually like me."

Paul smiled. "No worries. She's just cranky because she's tired. She'll be out like the ole light in a few."

Theo nodded. Frankie got fussy too when he was over-tired.

He led the way inside the cabin and into his office. Paul set the car seat on the floor next to his chair. When Paul removed his cowboy hat and set it on the table beside him, Theo could see the shadows under the man's eyes. He looked exhausted. He'd probably been up all night with the baby, just like Jace used to be when Frankie was under six months.

"Help yourself to coffee or juice," Theo said, gesturing at the refreshment credenza he always set up for these interviews along the back wall. There was a single-serving coffee maker and all the fixings and a small fridge with cold beverages. Theo used to have a basket of treats, like chips and pretzels and nuts, but after one rancher had crunched his way through the interview, Theo hadn't made that rookie mistake again.

Paul made himself a cup of coffee and sat down, check-ing on Maya, who wasn't asleep yet but was about to be. Her eyes kept fluttering closed.

Theo played the intro he'd recorded several days ago, the new rancher perking up with excitement as Theo discussed the Newton Ranch's history and how meaningful it was to Paul and his wife to continue the legacy. He'd worked at his grandfather's ranch from a young age and hoped to return the place to the successful, though small, cattle operation it had been when his grandfather was younger.

Theo got through one question before Maya began fuss-ing. He stopped recording and let Paul try to settle his baby daughter. But she started crying.

"Sorry about this," Paul said, taking the baby from the car seat and holding her against him. He rocked her in his arms until her eyes got heavy again, then attempted to put her back in the car seat.

She screamed. Loudly.

"Oh, darn," Paul said. "This might not work today."

"It's no trouble. We can try again tomorrow if that's good for you."

Paul nodded and seemed disappointed. He bounced Maya in his arms. She screeched again, batting her fists. "I'd better get her home."

Theo watched the new dad take the moment to caress the baby's hair and coo at her a bit, telling her it was okay, that she was fine, that they were going back to see Mama. Paul seemed torn between loving his daughter and wishing he could do the podcast. Theo would make sure they got it done, if not for release this week, then for next week.

He assured Paul of that and watched the man leave, carefully holding the car seat. Theo could hear the baby crying even once Paul was at his truck, struggling to latch it into the back.

Theo watched out the window and sighed.

This was exactly what he didn't want for his own life. An opportunity ripped away because the baby had to come first, plain and simple.

He was supposed to go over to Bethany's tonight for dinner and to watch a movie. But he was afraid all his concerns and worries would manifest in him acting like a jerk—being quiet or distant.

And because she deserved much better than that, he'd tell her the truth, that he was very…uncomfortable with what he was facing in five months.

But the worst part was setting up Bethany to believe one thing and then blindsiding her.

And breaking her heart.

He couldn't bear that.

His phone pinged with a text. His dad.

Up for taking a shift with Thunderstorm tonight? He's got some stomach issues and the vet said I need to watch him overnight.

Of course, he texted back. The quarter horse was one of his dad's favorites.

He'd miss his night with Bethany, but this was for the best. He needed a little time to think. A lot of time. And since tomorrow night was Stanley Sanchez's bachelor party, he'd have tomorrow night too to figure out how he felt.

What he wanted.

You think you know what you want…

Stanley's psychic fiancée's words came back to him. At least he understood more now that he didn't seem to know what he wanted anymore. He couldn't imagine saying goodbye to Bethany, but she was a package deal. So…

What is meant to happen will…

The problem was that his understanding of how that applied to him kept changing.

Darn it, Bethany thought, flopping down on her sofa and putting her phone on the coffee table.

Theo had been quiet all day. Usually he texted a couple of times, just cute little things—to ask if she had any cravings he could fulfill, adding a winking emoji and then a string of foods, like pie or a burger or a taco. But today, not a single text.

And just a second ago, he'd called to say he wouldn't be able to come over tonight, after all, that his dad had asked for his help in watching over a sick horse in the stables.

Theo hadn't asked her to join him. Not that taking an overnight shift in a barn sounded like fun for a pregnant woman who got backaches even from her extremely comfortable bed, but still…

Maybe he was having second thoughts about their dating.

After a few nights spent together, having a great time, having great sex, he probably had started thinking about what was coming.

A baby.

A night off to get his head together was probably a good thing.

But tomorrow night he'd be busy for hours at Stanley's bachelor party, so she wouldn't see him until the day after.

That might be a little too much time to think. She was only half joking about that, she realized.

She sighed and took a sip of her iced tea. She'd go over her song list for the Cobbs-Sanchez wedding, do a final practice of the song for their first dance, a '50s ballad that gave her goose bumps every time she heard the original.

For the next hour, she worked on the song, ate cereal with a handful of blueberries tossed in for dinner since that was what she was craving, and then took a shower. She'd just dressed in her at-home uniform of maternity yoga pants and a T-shirt when her doorbell rang.

Her heart soared. Theo?

She ran to the intercom and pressed it. "Hello?"

She was so excited to see him. Maybe he was stopping by for a kiss before his night away from her.

Aww.

"Bethany?" came a familiar voice that was *not* Theo Abernathy's. "It's Rexx."

She gasped. Rexx? *What?*

She sucked in a breath. And buzzed him up.

What the heck was he doing here? Wasn't he living in Colorado now? With his fiancée? Maybe he'd somehow heard through the grapevine that she was pregnant and had done the math and realized it might be his baby.

She pulled open the door. When she saw Rexx Winters standing there, she honestly wondered how she'd ever spent a night with him. She felt absolutely nothing for him—not even the connection of being parents. He looked different too—he'd cut his wild, rocker-like mane and now kind of looked like a bank teller with his short, neatly brushed blond hair and button-down shirt tucked into khaki pants. The Rexx she'd known had worn silver rings on all his fingers and thrift-store velvet shirts.

"It's good to see you," he said.

She nodded—feeling so awkward. She'd wanted to get in touch with him, and now here he magically was. But suddenly, sharing her joyous news with someone who seemed like a stranger and yet was her child's father... well, it just seemed odd.

"Come on in," she said. "Can I get you something to drink?"

"If you have a beer, that would be great."

"Actually, I'm plumb out of all alcoholic beverages," she said. "Because of this," she added, pointing with both hands at her baby bump.

He looked at her belly. Understanding did not dawn.

Rexx was a smart guy—immature but smart. And clearly he had things on his mind. Maybe he thought she'd just gained a little weight and wasn't drinking to save calories.

She inwardly sighed. "I'm *pregnant*."

His brown eyes widened. "Pregnant? Wow. You don't look too far along."

"Almost five months," she said. And waited.

Nothing. No math computing.

"I called you a couple of months ago," she said. "But you barely let me get a word in and then ended the call before I could tell you my news. *Our* news," she added.

Now his eyes bugged out. "Wait. Are you saying I'm the father?" he asked.

"Yes." She launched into the story, how she assumed there was a tear in the condom that he hadn't noticed. That she'd gone to a fertility clinic only to find out she was already pregnant. She told him she'd tried to call him last week but had discovered he'd changed his number.

He had the decency to look sheepish. "Well, Bethany, I've come at exactly the right time. We have five months to get ready. To work on being a couple. That's awesome."

Huh? "What do you mean—a couple? You're *engaged*. You live in Colorado."

He sighed and moved to the sofa and sat down. "She dumped me. She said I wasn't acting the way I did when we first met. All gaga, I guess. She wanted me to give up being a musician, so I got a full-time job doing data entry for a bank, but she said it wasn't bringing in enough money." He frowned. "I really thought we were gonna be forever, you know? I tried so hard to change for her."

"That explains the hair and clothes," she said with a gentle smile.

"Yeah. She liked my old look, but then once things got serious between us, she wanted me to look more professional." He sighed. "But now that you're pregnant, I mean, now that I *know*...let's give this a go."

She appreciated the sentiment. But...and there were a lot of buts where they were concerned, she and Rexx had never been a match. They both had known that when they'd had that unexpected one-night stand. No chemistry. No real attraction even. They'd been two lonely people who'd had a little too much to drink and had been away on a gig. And afterward, when she'd been ready to write him off as anything other than a one-night stand, her bandmate who'd she'd not been close to, she'd beaten herself up about it. That maybe her quickness to say no, to walk away, was something she had to work on. She'd been willing to give him a chance. But then he'd turned the tables on her.

"Rexx, I'm glad I was finally able to tell you about the baby. But the truth is that I'm in love with someone else. I hope you'll be in the baby's life, but we can't be a couple."

He leaned his head back against the sofa. "Yeah, I know we're not really a match. Jeez, me a father? I never really saw that for myself, but if I'm gonna be a dad, then I want to be there as much as I can."

"As much as you can?" she repeated.

"Well, you know, birthdays. Christmas."

Gotcha. She mentally shook her head. "Look, Rexx, you just found out some startling news. Why don't you sleep on it and we can talk tomorrow? You can figure out how you want to coparent." She was so relieved that her baby would grow up knowing his father, that even if Rexx was going to be more absentee and there for just birthdays and holidays than truly involved in his child's life, at least he wouldn't be a big question mark.

He nodded and stood. "I appreciate that."

She walked him to the door.

"I'll text you tomorrow. You'll have my new number. Maybe we can have dinner tomorrow night and talk things out? Here, so we have privacy to really be open with each other, if that's okay. I remember you always liked Pasta-bilities. You can text me your order and I'll pick it up on the way over."

"Sounds good," she said. "See you tomorrow."

The moment she closed the door behind him, she let out a breath. *Whoa. Talk about unexpected.*

The whole thing almost made her think that anything was possible. Did that mean that even Theo Abernathy could be ready by the time she had her baby?

The truth is that I'm in love with someone else...

She absolutely was. And hoped with all her heart, everything inside her, that Theo would want to be a part of her life—and her future.

Chapter Seventeen

The good news was that Thunderstorm had pulled through just fine *and* that Theo had gotten to spend some quality time with his dad. The two of them had spent the night in the stables with the horse, in the large sick-bay stall, and they'd talked about so much—from the ranch to how Jace and Billy and now Robin had all found love. Asa Abernathy had shared that he and Bonnie were sure that Theo and Stacy, the last two holdouts of their five children, were soon to find their own loves and settle down.

And though Theo hadn't planned on opening up to his dad about his love life, he'd found himself pouring out what was going on with him and Bethany McCreery. How it made no sense that he could be so attracted—on every level—to a pregnant woman when he wasn't ready to be a father and couldn't see that for himself for years yet.

Instead of lecturing Theo about it being time to grow up, that he'd sowed his oats and all that, his father had counseled him with one line of advice: "Just follow your heart."

There was still a big but there, though. Where Bethany was concerned, he could only follow his heart to a certain point. And that point was the day before she gave birth and became a mother. Maybe as the months went on, he'd get more and more used to the idea of fatherhood. That was possible. He just couldn't see it.

But he missed her. So much.

This morning, he'd sent her a text to ask how she was doing, if he could bring anything by before he got busy in the ranch office. She'd texted back that she was fine, just a little backachy, and her mom was stopping by with not only breakfast and her favorite home fries from the diner, but a massage gun specifically for pregnant women.

Theo had missed her terribly all day. He wished he could see her tonight, but he had special plans. He wouldn't miss Stanley Sanchez's bachelor party for the world. All the Abernathy men would be there, including his uncle and cousins, which added to the fun; they were extended family now because of Robin's marriage to Dylan Sanchez.

When Theo arrived right on time at the Library, the restaurant in Bronco Valley owned by Dylan's sister Camilla, the bachelor party was just getting underway in a large private room behind the main dining room. He saw Stanley, in his trademark leather vest and bolo tie, and tonight a sombrero, surrounded by a small group, including Theo's brothers. Theo liked this restaurant. He'd heard that Camilla had offered to hold the wedding reception here, but apparently the happy couple had opted for the park, especially because the guest list was huge.

He extended his hand to congratulate Stanley, and the warm, kind man pulled him into a hug, careful not to spill his glass of sangria.

Theo was surprised when his father raised his own glass of sangria and tapped against it with a spoon to get everyone's attention. Asa then gave a brief speech about how Stanley and Winona had inspired the entire town, that their love was legendary.

Theo was moved by his father's words, and a look around the room told him everyone else was too.

Stanley then raised his glass. "I'm getting married! To love!"

A cheer went up, and there was much clapping and many wolf whistles. His guests joined him in the toast.

"I love my Winona so much," Stanley said, tears brimming in his eyes. "How could I have gotten so lucky to have a second chance at love?"

"Because you're the best, *Tío*," Dylan said. "You deserve all the happiness in the universe."

"I never thought you'd beat me to the altar!" Stanley said, making everyone laugh. "One surprise after another in this family."

Theo's uncle and Dylan's father tapped their glasses to give a speech, and a few others did as well, including Winona's great-grandson, Evan Cruise. Stanley had his hand over his heart, clearly moved by all the warm wishes and everyone's love and respect.

Once the toasts were over, Stanley sidled up to Theo and suddenly slung an arm around his shoulder. "I guess you'll be next. You and that lovely wedding singer, Bethany. Such a voice!"

"I could listen to her sing forever," Theo said.

Stanley nodded. "Marry that woman before someone beats you to it."

Theo swallowed. "It's not that simple."

Stanley lifted his chin and pointed a finger at him. "Oh, it is. Do you love her?"

Theo hadn't been expecting that question. This was all

too much. He didn't respond, taking a long drink of his sangria instead.

Stanley shook his head with a mock frown. He waved his hand dismissively in the air. "Love is wasted on the young."

Theo's dad, in earshot, grinned at Stanley. "Yeah, sometimes I think it is," he said, patting Stanley on the back.

"Hey, don't include me and Jace in that," Billy said with a smile. "We're both engaged."

Stanley laughed. "*Some* young people spend too much time overanalyzing things instead of *feeling*, instead of following their hearts." He pointedly looked at Theo.

Asa's eyes lit up. "Exactly what I told my son last night."

Theo quickly downed the rest of his sangria.

"Hey, let's face facts," Jace said. "Theo isn't all that young."

That got a big laugh out of the group.

Theo looked at his brothers, both family men, both so happy.

Both so in love, like Stanley.

And me, he thought with a clarity that hit him right in the chest.

Whoa. Wow.

I love Bethany McCreery.

A lot.

He could actually feel his heart shifting in his chest. Could feel it cracking open. He swallowed against the lump in his throat. He loved Bethany. He loved her so much.

And he understood now that he always had. From the moment he'd been mesmerized by her voice and her face and her body as she sang on stage at her brother's wedding.

She'd had him at the first note.

He'd been so focused on what he'd be giving up that he hadn't spent enough time thinking about what he had. Why would he ever want to be free to jet off to Rome for the best pasta in the world when he'd be more content to pick up dinner for two from Pastabilities and eat in the living room while watching a rom-com with the woman he loved? Bethany.

Who was pregnant.

Bethany was a package deal, and because he loved her, he wanted everything she was. That included the baby-to-be.

Goose bumps ran up his arms and across the nape of his neck.

He *would* have almost five months to get used to the idea that he'd be a father to her baby. But with Bethany at his side, he'd be happy to give up everything. Actually, there was nothing to give up. If he had Bethany, he had it all.

He'd be ready for fatherhood because she was going to be a mother. It really *was* that simple.

Because he loved her with all his heart.

He'd always been aware that his brothers had made it work—balancing family life with their responsibilities to the Bonnie B. He'd talk to them about how they handled it, how they managed to give all of themselves to both. If they could do it, he could.

They were Abernathys.

When the party wound down, he pulled Stanley aside.

"I owe you a big thanks," he told the man of honor. "Because I have an answer to your earlier question. I *do* love the wedding singer." He laughed and shook his head. "Turns out I knew it all along."

"So why are you still here?" Stanley asked with a wink.

Theo hugged the wise man and raced out.

Theo couldn't wait to get to Bethany. To tell her that he was ready for anything life with her brought him, including a baby. Fatherhood. For the next eighteen years and the rest of their lives.

He got in his car and drove over to Bethany's apartment, so excited to share his epiphany. To share his *life* with Bethany and the baby.

He pressed the buzzer, and when he heard her say, "Hello?" he felt butterflies in his stomach.

"It's me, Theo. I have something to tell you."

She didn't respond for a moment. Then the buzzer sounded, and he rushed in, taking the stairs two at a time, needing to get to her as soon as he could.

She opened the door and he was bursting with his *I love you*. But her expression stopped him cold. Something was wrong.

Bethany looked...uncomfortable.

She opened the door wider, and Theo saw there was a man sitting on the sofa, who suddenly stood. It took Theo a moment to realize the guy was the same one from the photo of the band on Bethany's mantel. With much shorter hair.

Rexx.

The baby's father.

What was going on here?

He noticed that on the coffee table was a takeout bag from Pastabilities—the restaurant where he and Bethany had had their first date. Not that he had called it that. But that was exactly what it had been.

And now she was having Pastabilities takeout with Rexx. Her child's father.

He saw Bethany lean over to Rexx and whisper something to him. What, he had no idea.

His blood ran cold. What the hell was going on?

Theo froze. Were they getting back together?

No. No, no, no. This couldn't be happening. He'd finally realized that he was ready for fatherhood, that he could be the man Bethany needed.

His chest ached and his gut burned.

Rexx came over, his hand extended. Theo didn't shake it. Couldn't.

The guy dropped his hand. "I'm Rexx Winters. I'll say my piece, since Bethany just told me that you two were involved and there were some unresolved issues. I found out last night that Bethany is pregnant—with my child. And with some time to think, I realize that I *do* want a second chance, despite our differences. I want us to be a family."

Bethany's mouth dropped open. She stared at Rexx, then turned to Theo, about to say something.

But Theo didn't wait to hear what it was—likely that no one was more surprised than she was to hear Rexx say those words, and that for the baby's sake, she and Rexx should be together.

That was true, wasn't it? Family was everything. If her baby could have his parents together, an intact family, wasn't that worth fighting for?

He'd lost her. He'd just discovered that she was his everything, that he wanted to be part of her family. And he had to let her go. For her sake. For the baby's sake.

His heart cracking in two, Theo rushed down the stairs and into his car and got the hell out of there.

Bethany was still in a state of shock. That Theo had unexpectedly come over, that he'd said he had something to tell her.

And that Rexx had so outrageously interfered. What the hell had he been thinking?

What was Theo going to say? She really wanted to know. That he couldn't keep seeing her? That he knew in his heart he didn't want to be a dad in five months, that nothing had changed? That he was sorry?

The apartment door was still open, the downstairs door softly clicking into its locked position behind Theo.

She closed her eyes for a moment, trying to make sense of what had just happened. Rexx had arrived just ten minutes ago with takeout from Pastabilities and had told her he'd thought long and hard about the big news that he was going to be a father. But then the buzzer had rung before she'd had a chance to say anything.

"Sorry not sorry that I messed that up for you," Rexx said—selfishly. "We can work on our relationship for the baby's sake."

Bethany shook her head. "Rexx, first of all, you *should* be sorry. Very sorry. I care about that man. And you had no right to say one word to him." She was fuming. And wondering what Theo was thinking right now.

Rexx winced and peered at her. "Huh. I guess I am sorry." His shoulders sunk. "No, forget the guessing. I *am* sorry, truly. I know I have to learn to think first, talk second. But I was just hoping—"

"Its a nice thought," she interrupted. "And of course you can be in the baby's life. That's very important to me. But like you said last night, we're not a match. We never were. And there's nothing to work toward. We don't belong together."

He sighed hard and sat back down on the sofa. "Yeah,

I know. I'm just really broken up about losing Veronica. I guess I'm rebounding."

Bethany forced herself to stay calm and not lose her temper. Rexx was immature. He didn't have feelings for her. He'd gotten dumped and seen an immediate in for a relationship with her. He'd be gone in a few weeks when he met someone new, child or no child.

"Look, Rexx. You're this baby's father, and you're always welcome in our lives. I do hope you'll take your responsibilities seriously. This little person in here," she added, patting her belly, "is counting on you to be their dad, you know?"

He sucked in a breath. "When you put it like that…" He frowned and looked kind of scared.

She had a feeling that Rexx would fall in love with someone else pretty soon, and maybe that person, along with impending fatherhood, would end up directing Rexx to take life and his responsibilities seriously. She sure hoped so.

Rexx got up. "Thanks for being you, Bethany. You're all right."

Bethany forced herself not to roll her eyes. He was being nice and sincere, but boy, did he have a ways to go in life—and he was in his early thirties.

He reached into the Pastabilities bag and took out a container and a wrapped set of plastic flatware. "My chicken parm and linguine," he said. "Your pasta primavera and garlic bread are in there with the extra side of grated Parmesan cheese you asked for."

"Thanks, Rexx." She didn't have an appetite anymore, not even for the garlic bread.

"I hope I didn't mess anything up with Theo. Go get your guy," he said.

Huh. That was kind. Maybe there was hope for Rexx yet.

They said their goodbyes, and she felt good about Rexx growing up. She wouldn't hold her breath, but she had a feeling he'd try.

Once he left, she dropped down on the sofa—all this was way too much to process. She sat for a few minutes, then got up and put the bag with her dinner into the fridge.

She found herself drawn to the nursery and went inside. The bassinet Theo had bought and assembled waited in a corner for her baby, the mobile so sweet above it.

I love you, Theo Abernathy, she thought, her gaze going to the pair of baby booties on the dresser.

I want to raise my child with you at my side.

Maybe he'd come tonight to tell her he couldn't do that.

But until she heard it from him, there was still hope. The past few days they'd been a couple—not talking about the future at all. The subject of her impending parenthood hadn't come up.

Maybe these past few days he'd had that change of heart.

She hurried downstairs and into her car and drove over to the Bonnie B, hoping Theo was home. When she pulled up at his cabin-mansion, lights were on inside, and relief flooded her.

She knocked, and the sound of his footsteps approaching had her so nervous. *Please, please, please*, she whispered to the fates of the universe.

Theo opened the door and looked surprised to see her. "I thought you'd be deciding on names or something with Rexx."

He looked so hurt, so…heartbroken that Bethany realized they really *might* have a chance.

"Theo, I'm not going to be with Rexx. Surely you know that."

He stared at her. "But he said he wanted to be a family."

"And I want to be a family—with *you*. You're the man I love."

He looked away for a moment. "The connection between the two of you has to be powerful, Bethany. In a week, a month, with the two of you spending time together as parents-to-be, you'll probably realize that having such a monumental thing in common is enough. And you'll get back together."

What was he talking about? "Theo, that's not going to happen. I don't have feelings for Rexx. Yes, I hope he'll step up and be an active parent to his child, but that's as far as it goes."

"You could change your mind, Bethany. And I don't want to stand in your way."

She stared at him, trying to understand. "Is this an excuse? To make it easier on you to walk away from me?" Tears pricked her eyes. "Theo, when you came over tonight, you said you had something to tell me. What was it?"

"It doesn't matter now," he said. "We need to say goodbye, Bethany. I need to let you go."

No. No, no, no. This couldn't be happening.

Her heart was breaking. The ache in her chest hurt so badly that she touched her hand to the spot as tears pooled in her eyes.

Something was happening inside Theo that she didn't know how to reach.

"Theo," she began, but she could tell by the look on his

face that he'd shut down. He was done talking, and there was no getting through to him.

Not tonight, anyway.

She didn't want to give up on this man, but she couldn't keep fighting for him when there was no getting through to him.

She couldn't keep giving him more time when she had so little left to give.

Even if it meant she'd lose him for good.

Chapter Eighteen

A week later, Bethany hadn't heard from Theo. Somehow, she'd managed to get through three weddings, each so different—a backyard, a campsite, and the private room of the Library, where she knew Stanley Sanchez had had his bachelor party the night she'd seen Theo last. Bethany had sung her heart out with her band, her own heartache adding a new dimension of yearning and authenticity to her voice that had actually earned her a couple of standing ovations. She'd had many folks come up to her and ask if she and her band were available to perform on certain dates. Her job this past week had been bittersweet, to say the least.

Today was yet another wedding, one she'd been waiting for, one the entire town of Bronco was so excited for: Winona Cobbs would say I do to her handsome groom, Stanley Sanchez. The ceremony was taking place in the Bronco Valley Church. A huge reception, to which hundreds had been invited, would follow in the park, and everything from the necessary permit to the bride's gown to the tents and food and flowers had all been comped by various businesses and townspeople who adored the elderly couple. Had anyone in Bronco not been inspired by Winona and Stanley, moved by their stories, their romance, their love?

Bethany sure had. And today, she'd put aside her hurt, her tears, and the surety that Theo Abernathy was out of her life for good to share in that love between the couple.

Just a couple of days ago she'd listened to his latest podcast just so she could hear his voice, feel connected to him. Tears in her eyes, she'd been riveted by the story of a young ranching family, the Newtons, with a three-month-old baby. In Theo's introduction, which he'd said he'd revised and rerecorded three times until he got it right, he'd discussed how the young couple's ranching life wasn't easy, that they were trying to get a failing farm out of the red, and that their sweet baby girl, who was colicky, gave them all the extra motivation they needed when they were exhausted and worried that they wouldn't succeed.

"Our child stands for possibilities, for love, for hope," Paul Newton had said. "And to secure our baby's legacy and lineage, my wife and I will never give up, even when we've both been awake all night with nighttime feedings. Even when we're trying to soothe a colicky baby when we have a small herd to care for, the work of the ranch never finished."

"Because we love each other. We love our little family. our little ranch," his wife had said.

"I have no doubt these young ranchers—little family, little ranch, but with the biggest *hearts* will not only survive, but succeed," Theo had commented.

Bethany had been moved to tears by their story.

She'd been so surprised when the baby, Maya, had made her podcast debut with quite a screechy cry, Theo adding that this was life in all its messy glory.

"Its beautiful and blessed messy glory," he'd said.

When Theo had signed off for the week, she'd gone straight to Hey, Baby and bought Maya a stuffed animal and dropped it in the couple's mailbox with a note about how she admired them so much and how their story helped her know she'd always be okay because her love for her baby would guide her. She wished she'd been able to give more to the young couple, but Bethany had no doubt donations and toys and ranch equipment would come pouring in for the Newtons.

Now, Bethany stood with her mike beside the organist, doing a quick rehearsal of the song the couple had chosen for Winona to walk down the aisle. The wedding would begin in a half hour, and already so many people were milling about outside. Bethany had seen the Sanchez family, including Stanley, who looked so handsome and proud and happy in his tux and his elegant sombrero and bolo tie. Winona's relatives were here, corralled by her proud daughter Beatrix. Others began streaming in—there were newlyweds Dylan and Robin holding hands as they kissed and then joined a group of Dylan's relatives back out on the church's large porch. Ryan Taylor and Gabrielle Hammond came in and admired the beautiful stained glass windows as they chatted with Shep Dalton and Rylee Parker. A few other Daltons were with them, but Bethany could never remember all their names. On the porch, she could see the Burris family had gathered, including Ross and his bride, Celeste.

"Hi, Aunt Bethany!" a chorus of little voices said, and she glanced out the door to see her treasure trove of nieces and nephews waving, the adorable brood all dressed up.

Her brother was in his suit and Stetson, and Elizabeth looked so pretty in her Western-style fancy dress.

Bethany waved back with a big smile. Twenty minutes until the music would start and the wedding would begin. That she'd cry her eyes out wasn't in doubt. That was what waterproof mascara and strong tissues were for. She only hoped she could get through the emotional song the couple had chosen to accompany the bride down the aisle without sobbing.

As Dylan and Robin went back out onto the porch, she got a glimpse of Theo in his own suit and Stetson talking with a group of Abernathys, his siblings and cousins.

Her heart squeezed, and she winced from the ache, tears already forming.

Suddenly she felt a hand on her shoulder and turned to find Penny Smith, the mayor's wife, looking at her with compassion. There was no hiding the heartbreak on her face, Bethany knew.

"Bethany, honey, will you turn around for a moment?" Penny asked.

Bethany looked at her, not understanding. Then she saw Penny reaching up to her neck to take off her pearl necklace.

Bethany gasped softly. Everyone in town knew the pearl necklace was rumored to have magical properties. It brought love to anyone who wore it.

She turned and felt the beautiful necklace drape around her neck, Penny's hands patting both shoulders.

"There," Penny said. "Wear it for the ceremony. It goes so beautifully with your pale blue dress."

Bethany took Penny's hand and gave it a squeeze. "Thank you," she barely managed to say.

Penny squeezed her hand back and then joined her husband, who was talking to a group of the Taylor clan. Daphne and her husband, Evan, Winona's great-grandson, suddenly moved up near where Bethany stood beside the organ, whispering to each other and both checking their phones.

Bethany's heart lurched when Evan looked up from his phone and whispered, "Cold feet?" She then heard Daphne say that Winona wasn't even here yet when she was supposed to be getting ready in the anteroom.

Stanley came in then with Beatrix and they rushed over to Daphne and Evan, everyone looking concerned but Stanley. Apparently, Beatrix had planned to drive her mother to the church a half hour before the ceremony so that Winona could put on the finishing touches in the anteroom, but Winona, who'd still been in her robe, had told her she'd walk over since the church was close to their house.

She hadn't.

"My bride will be here," Stanley insisted, straightening his bolo tie. He lifted his chin. "Winona is a free spirit, but we've been through so much together, especially these past six months. She'll be here soon, I'm very sure. She'd never leave me standing at altar."

That seem to brighten the group's expressions. But a look at Beatrix told Bethany that she was worried.

And ten minutes later, there was still no sign of the bride.

Winona wasn't responding to calls or texts. Evan had gone to check Winona's psychic shop at his Bronco Ghost Tours business, but he'd texted his wife that Winona wasn't there or anywhere on the property.

Where was the bride-to-be?

Bethany's heart lurched as she looked over at Stanley, nervously pacing by the stage now, several members of the Sanchez family trying to comfort him.

Was Winona not going to show up? Bethany couldn't believe it. The dear woman had to just be running late. Perhaps she'd had a psychic prediction about her own wedding and knew she had to arrive twenty minutes late or something bad would happen. Bethany was clearly grasping at straws here.

If Winona would stay away from her own wedding to the man she loved, it reinforced for Bethany that Theo Abernathy wasn't ever coming for her.

The wedding guests were all outside now, since the ceremony was supposed to start a half hour ago and there seemed no point for everyone to sit in the pews, particularly the many children, who were getting antsy. The moment Theo had arrived at the church with his family, he'd seen Bethany standing at the front with the organist and for just a second he'd imagined she was his bride-to-be, that this was their wedding day. But no matter how much he loved her, no matter how much he'd changed and could now welcome her baby into his life, he wouldn't stand in her and Rexx's way.

As he stood with his brothers on the side yard, he wondered if Rexx was here, if he was Bethany's plus-one for the event. If, that was, there was going to *be* a wedding.

Theo, Billy, and Jace were all eyeing their sisters, Robin and Stacy, who were across the lawn with Dylan and his siblings, talking in low voices, all of them looking very worried.

"Dang," Billy said. "I did hear that Winona had cold

feet a couple months back, but at Stanley's bachelor party, there was no indication from him that there was any trouble between them."

"The trouble may be one-sided," Jace pointed out. "Winona's a first-time bride, even at her age. Maybe she's still just not ready, given all she's been through in her life."

Not ready. That was Theo's line for his entire relationship with Bethany McCreery. But when love hit him over the head so hard even he couldn't ignore it, he'd believed he was ready for the package deal he'd be blessed with. But then Rexx came back, and how could Theo interfere in that?

Ever since he'd interviewed Paul Newton, who'd again been on baby duty because his wife had had a bad cold, Theo had been so focused on the word *family*. His own. Bethany's. And now the sweet idea that Bethany, Rexx, and their baby could be a family too. Paul had rocked little Maya in his arms during the entire interview, which had been one of Theo's favorites. He often learned a lot while putting together an episode of *This Ranching Life*, but the life experiences and wisdom coming out of twenty-three-year-old Paul Newton's mouth had bowled him over. All Theo's listeners too, apparently, because the family had received so many donations and offers of help with the ranch that Theo had felt his eyes mist.

"I'm doing this for the baby," Paul had said. "Everything my wife and I do is for her and her present and future. For today and tomorrow. I care about the Newton Ranch, but it's Maya who gives my life a meaning and purpose."

Theo had gotten that knocked into his skull along the way, but now it was too late.

Across the lawn, he saw the Newton family, Paul holding Maya and standing beside his wife, with a big group of people. Paul smiled and waved at Theo, and he waved back, moved by how his podcast had touched not only the young family but affected so many others. And one day, maybe Theo would be holding a baby and recording at 3:00 a.m. He understood now that life was full of the unexpected and challenges and you had to make them work, but your heart would always guide you. If you let it.

He got now that that was what Stanley had been trying to say at his bachelor party.

But it was too late now.

"Winona will show up," Billy said now, looking around like they all were and hoping that a purple pickup truck would suddenly pull up to the church, Winona stepping out.

But no sound of a truck or car or limo could be heard.

"I don't get it," Jace said. "Winona and Stanley have both lost so much in their lives. And here they are, so in love, so happy. Why would she be afraid of that?"

"Because of how damned scary it is to risk loving anything or anyone to the point that you vow to honor it forever," Theo said, then froze for a moment as he realized that was how *he* felt. His chest ached and his stomach churned as the stark truth hit him.

He'd come around, only to walk away from Bethany so that she could be with a man she'd said flat out she didn't have feelings for. What the hell had he done?

"Kind of like how you broke up with Bethany because you're afraid," Jace said as though he could read Theo's mind. "Not of giving up your carefree life. Of getting your heart ripped out of your chest."

Billy nodded. "You're scared out of your mind that

Bethany and her baby will be taken from you. So you're not even trying."

He inwardly gasped. His brothers were right.

What had he done?

A better question was: Could he fix it before it was too late?

Winona Cobbs was now thirty-five minutes late to her own wedding. Bethany had no idea if the bride would show up. No one had heard from her. Not even Stanley.

Most of the families with children had walked over to the park just across the road because it had a playground and they could come back at a moment's notice. Sure, the kids' Sunday best outfits would be rumpled and maybe even dirty, but it was the ceremony and reception that counted, not a grass stain on a hem.

Bethany stood by the stained glass window at the front of the church, too afraid to go outside and see Theo. She couldn't bear it. To be that close and yet light-years away.

She touched the pearl necklace at her throat and felt her eyes mist up. The anniversary gift to mark thirty wonderful years of Rafferty and Penny Smith's marriage had brought together quite a few couples. But love always seemed to pass right by Bethany.

She'd been blessed with a baby who'd be here in just four and a half months, and Bethany was counting down the days. She would focus on taking good care of herself, eating well and taking her prenatal vitamins and signing up for Lamaze class—with her sister-in-law as her coach. Bethany had been so touched when Elizabeth had called the other day to make that offer.

Bethany might not be lucky in love, but she was rich in family.

"Bethany," called a familiar deep voice, and she whirled around.

Theo, looking so handsome in his suit and gray Stetson, stood at the church entrance. He took off his hat and held it against his chest.

She waited—for him to come closer, for him to say something. But for the moment, he just stood there looking at her.

Maybe to say his final goodbye.

He started walking toward her. His expression gave her pause; he didn't look particularly pained, like a man who was about to tear her heart out—again.

He stopped in front of her and reached for her hand. "I don't know where Winona is or why she isn't here, but I do know she is psychic. She told me that what's meant to happen will, and she was right. I was meant to go through all this—not thinking I wanted a family yet, losing you to the father of your baby—for me to realize I was making excuses."

Bethany gasped, hope suddenly soaring in her heart. What was he saying?

Theo took her other hand and looked right in her eyes. "My brothers helped knock into my head that I'm scared spitless of how I feel."

"And how *do* you feel?" she asked, hope blossoming in her chest.

"I love you, Bethany McCreery. So much. And I love this little one-to-be," he added, moving a hand to her belly.

"Oh, Theo," she said, smiling at how many times she'd yearned to hear those words. "I love you too."

"You told me you didn't have feelings for Rexx, that the two of you wouldn't be a couple, but I refused to listen. Once I opened up to the fact that I am ready to be a father, fear got a hold of me, and I used Rexx as an excuse to run. But I'm done with that. I'm here to stand by your side forever. To be a father figure to your child."

Bethany felt tears mist her eyes. "This may be someone else's wedding day, but it's become the happiest day of my life."

Theo kissed her, sweetly and tenderly, looking into her eyes with such love.

He glanced at the pearl necklace. "Why does that look so familiar?"

She smiled. "It's just something borrowed," she said.

"Well, it looks beautiful on you. *You* look beautiful."

She kissed him again and then touched the necklace, wondering if the pearls really did have magical powers or if the magic came from those, like her, who believed.

Love was everything. And it hadn't passed her by. She'd just had to wait for it.

One minute Theo was right in front of her, and the next, he was gone.

Because he'd gotten down on one knee. He pulled something out of his pocket—something very big and very twinkly.

Her hand flew to her mouth.

"Bethany McCreery, with the voice of an angel and the most beautiful heart, will you make me the happiest man alive by marrying me?"

Bethany was speechless for a moment. She could only nod, tears pooling in her eyes. Finally she found her voice. "Yes, yes, yes. I'll marry you."

Theo stood and slid the huge, twinkling ring on her finger. "Okay, this is not your real engagement ring. It's a placeholder, which I borrowed from my twin niece's dress-up box. It's a beauty but your ring will be real, like my love for you."

Bethany was so touched she couldn't speak.

"In fact, it was at Stanley's bachelor party that I realized that I'd always loved you. I'm ready for you and the baby. Ready for anything that comes our way."

Bethany smiled and looked at her toy ring, then at her handsome fiancé. She really hoped she wouldn't have to give this back because she treasured it. Her heart felt like it might burst with happiness. She hugged Theo, and for a few moments, they stood there by the stained glass window and the organ, embracing, knowing that they'd be together forever.

They both looked toward the door, and Bethany hoped she'd see Winona come walking through in a purple wedding gown, but there was no sign of her.

She had no idea what was going to happen with one of Bronco's great love stories. But she did know that her own was one for the storybooks.

* * * * *